Disney DuckTales

Facebook: **facebook.com/idwpublishing**
Twitter: **@idwpublishing**
YouTube: **youtube.com/idwpublishing**
Tumblr: **tumblr.idwpublishing.com**
Instagram: **instagram.com/idwpublishing**

ISBN: 978-1-68405-613-2   23 22 21 20   1 2 3 4

COVER ARTIST
MARCO GHIGLIONE

COVER COLORIST
DARIO CALABRIA

LETTERER
TOM B. LONG

SERIES ASSISTANT EDITOR
ANNI PERHEENTUPA

SERIES EDITOR
CHRIS CERASI

COLLECTION EDITORS
JUSTIN EISINGER
and ALONZO SIMON

COLLECTION DESIGNER
CLYDE GRAPA

Originally published as DUCKTALES issues #18–20.

Chris Ryall, President, Publisher, & CCO
John Barber, Editor-In-Chief
Cara Morrison, Chief Financial Officer
Matt Ruzicka, Chief Accounting Officer
David Hedgecock, Associate Publisher
Jerry Bennington, VP of New Product Development
Lorelei Bunjes, VP of Digital Services
Justin Eisinger, Editorial Director, Graphic Novels & Collections
Eric Moss, Senior Director, Licensing and Business Development

Ted Adams and Robbie Robbins, IDW Founders

Special thanks to Stefano Ambrosio, Stefano Attardi, Julie Dorris, Marco Ghiglione, Jodi Hammerwold, Behnoosh Khalili, Manny Mederos, Eugene Paraszczuk, Carlotta Quattrocolo, Roberto Santillo, Christopher Troise, and Camilla Vedove.

MONEY-GRUBBING HOOLIGANS FROM THE DEEP!

WRITER: JOE CARAMAGNA
ARTISTS: EMILIO URBANO AND GIANFRANCO FLORIO
COLORISTS: LUCIO DE GIUSEPPE AND KAWAII

FLINTHEART... MCDUCK?!?

WRITER: STEVE BEHLING
ARTISTS: EMILIO URBANO AND GIANFRANCO FLORIO
COLORISTS: GIUSEPPE FONTANA AND DARIO CALABRIA

SAGA OF THE SUPER INTERN!

WRITER: JOE CARAMAGNA
ARTISTS: LUCA USAI, CIRO CANGIALOSI, CRISTINA STELLA, AND DANILO LOIZEDDA
COLORISTS: KAWAII AND LUCIO DE GIUSEPPE

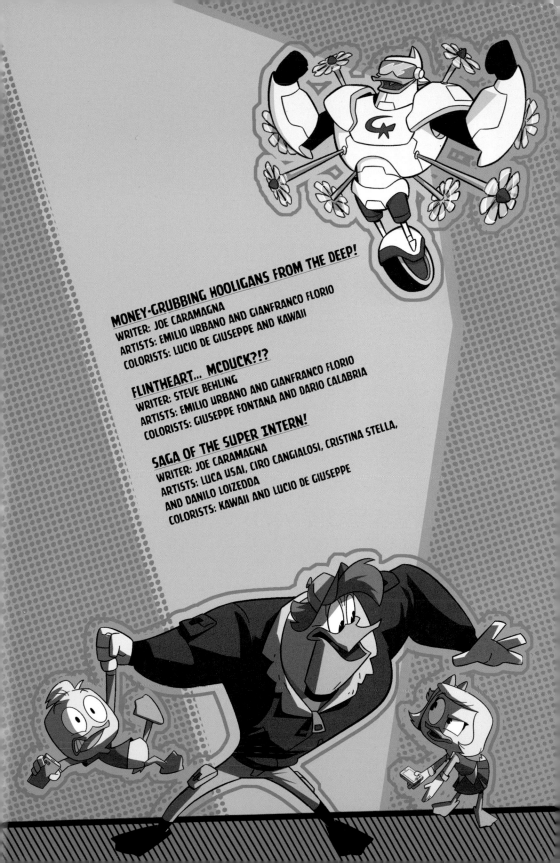

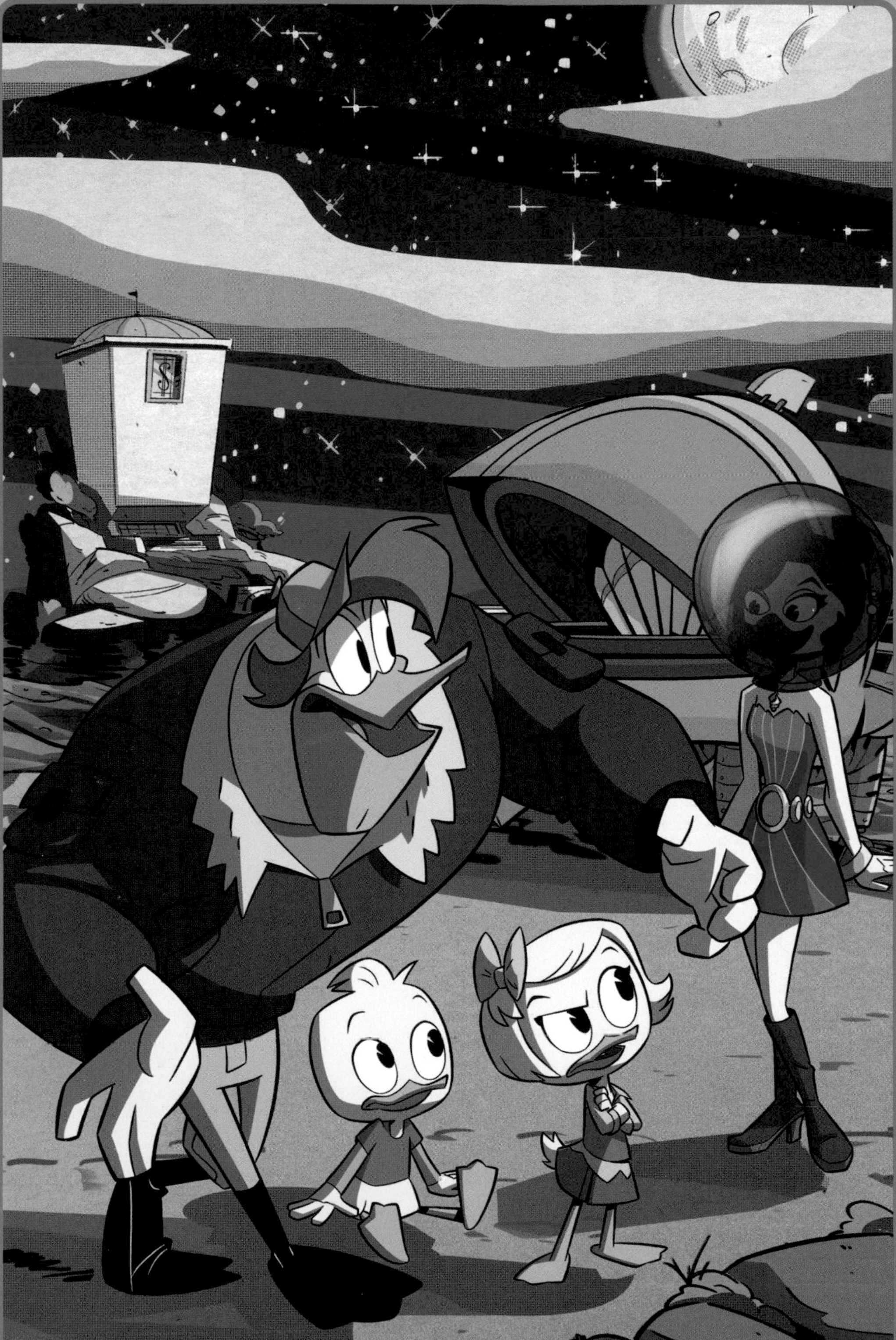

Art by Marco Ghiglione and Cristina Stella, Colors by Kawaii

Disney DuckTales

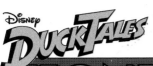

MONEY-GRUBBING HOOLIGANS FROM THE DEEP!

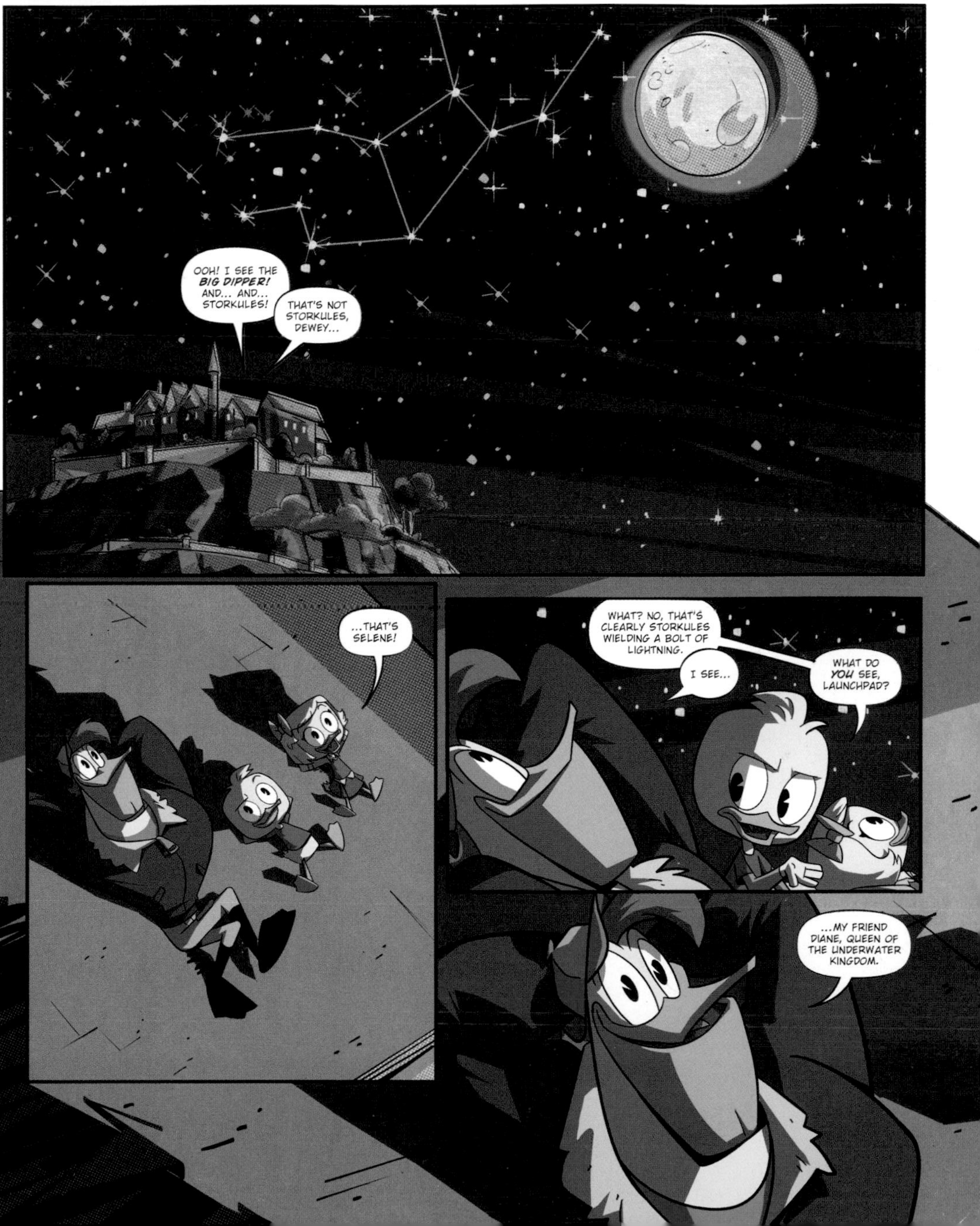
OOH! I SEE THE BIG DIPPER! AND... AND... STORKULES!
THAT'S NOT STORKULES, DEWEY...
...THAT'S SELENE!
WHAT? NO, THAT'S CLEARLY STORKULES WIELDING A BOLT OF LIGHTNING.
WHAT DO YOU SEE, LAUNCHPAD?
I SEE...
...MY FRIEND DIANE, QUEEN OF THE UNDERWATER KINGDOM.

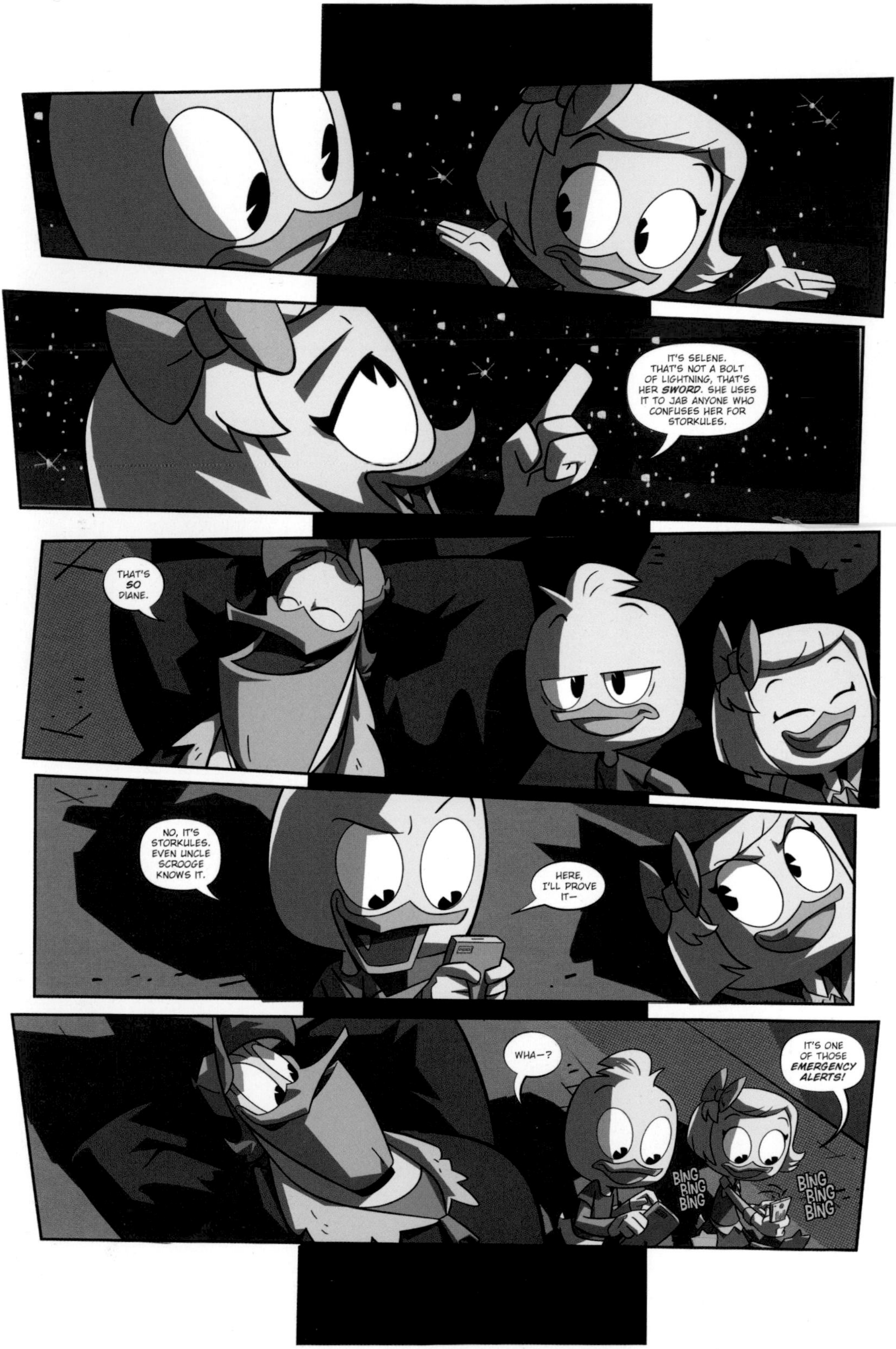
IT'S SELENE. THAT'S NOT A BOLT OF LIGHTNING, THAT'S HER SWORD. SHE USES IT TO JAB ANYONE WHO CONFUSES HER FOR STORKULES.
THAT'S SO DIANE.
NO, IT'S STORKULES. EVEN UNCLE SCROOGE KNOWS IT.
HERE, I'LL PROVE IT—
WHA—?
IT'S ONE OF THOSE EMERGENCY ALERTS!
BING BING BING
BING BING BING

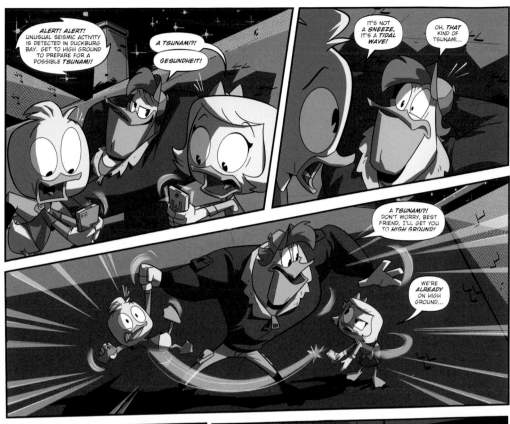

ALERT! ALERT! UNUSUAL SEISMIC ACTIVITY IS DETECTED IN DUCKBURG BAY. GET TO HIGH GROUND TO PREPARE FOR A POSSIBLE *TSUNAMI!*

A *TSUNAMI?!*
GESUNDHEIT!

IT'S NOT A *SNEEZE,* IT'S A *TIDAL WAVE!*

OH, *THAT* KIND OF TSUNAMI...

A *TSUNAMI?!* DON'T WORRY, BEST FRIEND, I'LL GET YOU TO *HIGH GROUND!*

WE'RE *ALREADY* ON HIGH GROUND...

...BUT *MR. McDUCK* ISN'T!"

MRS. BEAKLEY!

ANYTHING UNUSUAL HAPPENING IN THE WORLD?

WELL, THE SO-CALLED "SMARTEST OF THE SMARTIES" THINKS HIS *HOUSEKEEPER* IS HIS PERSONAL *NEWS BUREAU,* IF THAT'S WHAT YOU MEAN.

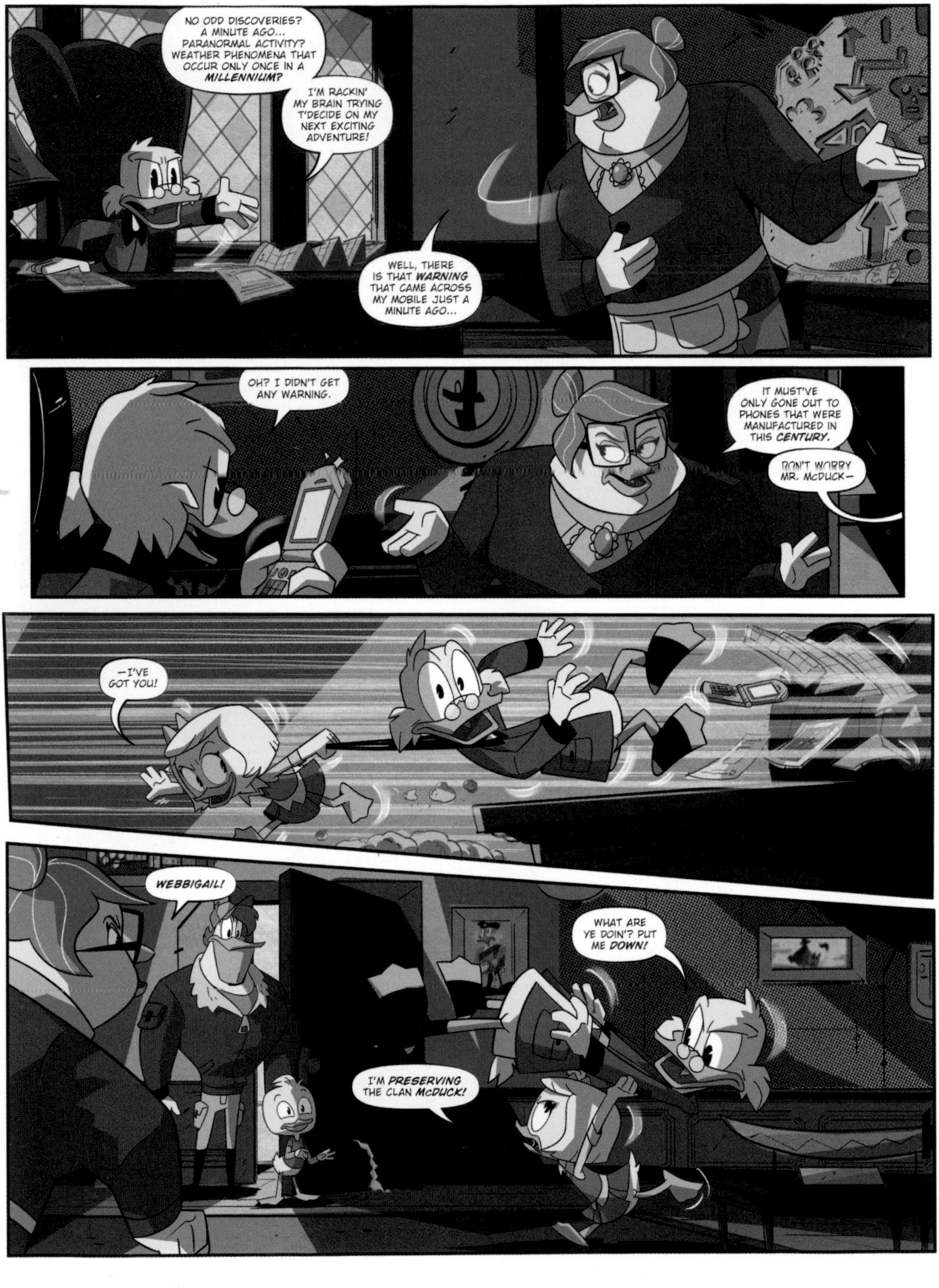
NO ODD DISCOVERIES? A MINUTE AGO... PARANORMAL ACTIVITY? WEATHER PHENOMENA THAT OCCUR ONLY ONCE IN A MILLENNIUM?
I'M RACKIN' MY BRAIN TRYING T'DECIDE ON MY NEXT EXCITING ADVENTURE!
WELL, THERE IS THAT WARNING THAT CAME ACROSS MY MOBILE JUST A MINUTE AGO...
OH? I DIDN'T GET ANY WARNING.
IT MUST'VE ONLY GONE OUT TO PHONES THAT WERE MANUFACTURED IN THIS CENTURY.
DON'T WORRY MR. McDUCK—
—I'VE GOT YOU!
WEBBIGAIL!
WHAT ARE YE DOIN'? PUT ME DOWN!
I'M PRESERVING THE CLAN McDUCK!

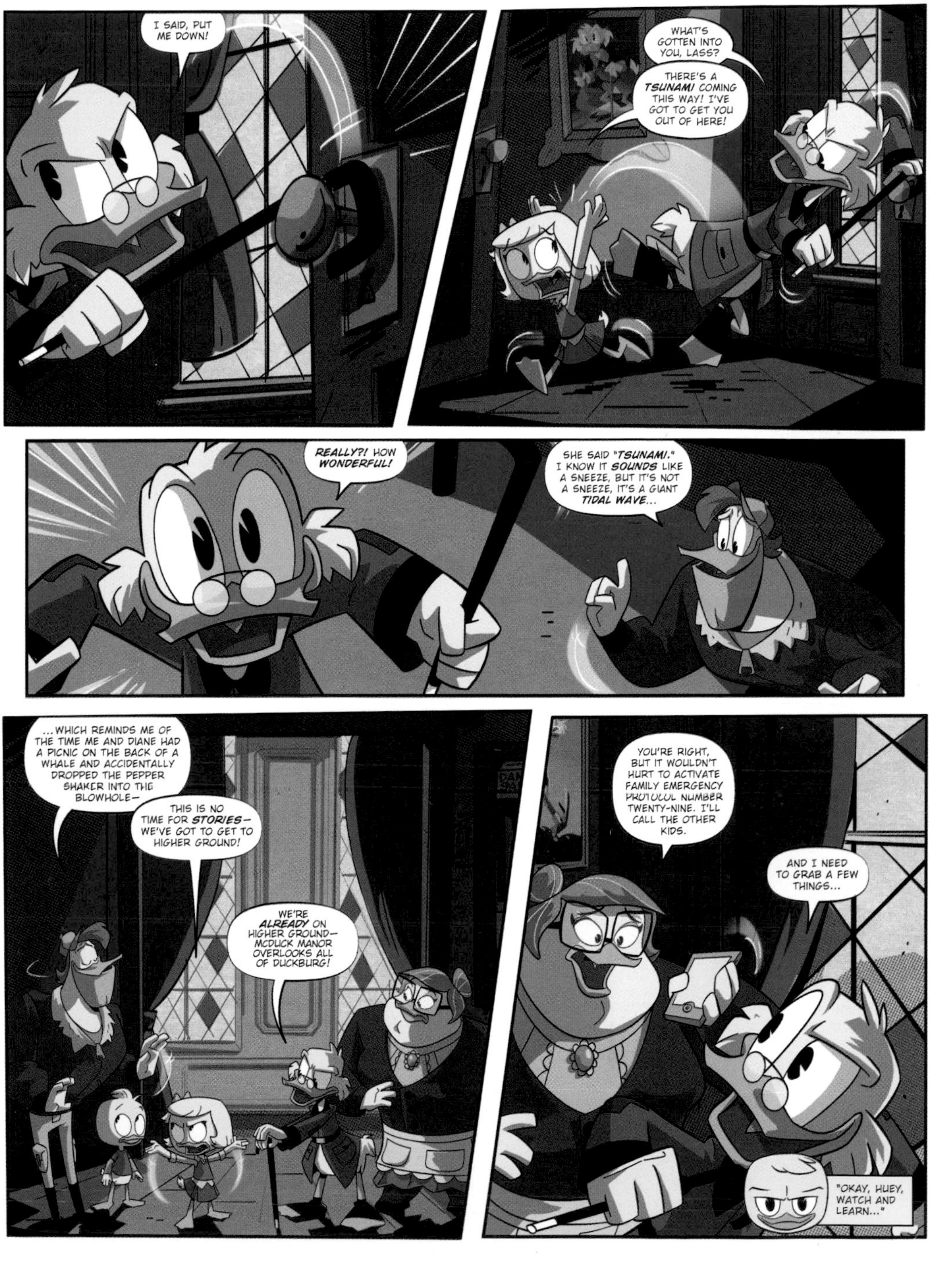
I SAID, PUT ME DOWN!
WHAT'S GOTTEN INTO YOU, LASS?
THERE'S A TSUNAMI COMING THIS WAY! I'VE GOT TO GET YOU OUT OF HERE!
REALLY?! HOW WONDERFUL!
SHE SAID "TSUNAMI." I KNOW IT SOUNDS LIKE A SNEEZE, BUT IT'S NOT A SNEEZE, IT'S A GIANT TIDAL WAVE...
...WHICH REMINDS ME OF THE TIME ME AND DIANE HAD A PICNIC ON THE BACK OF A WHALE AND ACCIDENTALLY DROPPED THE PEPPER SHAKER INTO THE BLOWHOLE—
THIS IS NO TIME FOR STORIES— WE'VE GOT TO GET TO HIGHER GROUND!
WE'RE ALREADY ON HIGHER GROUND— McDUCK MANOR OVERLOOKS ALL OF DUCKBURG!
YOU'RE RIGHT, BUT IT WOULDN'T HURT TO ACTIVATE FAMILY EMERGENCY PROTOCOL NUMBER TWENTY-NINE. I'LL CALL THE OTHER KIDS.
AND I NEED TO GRAB A FEW THINGS...
"OKAY, HUEY, WATCH AND LEARN..."

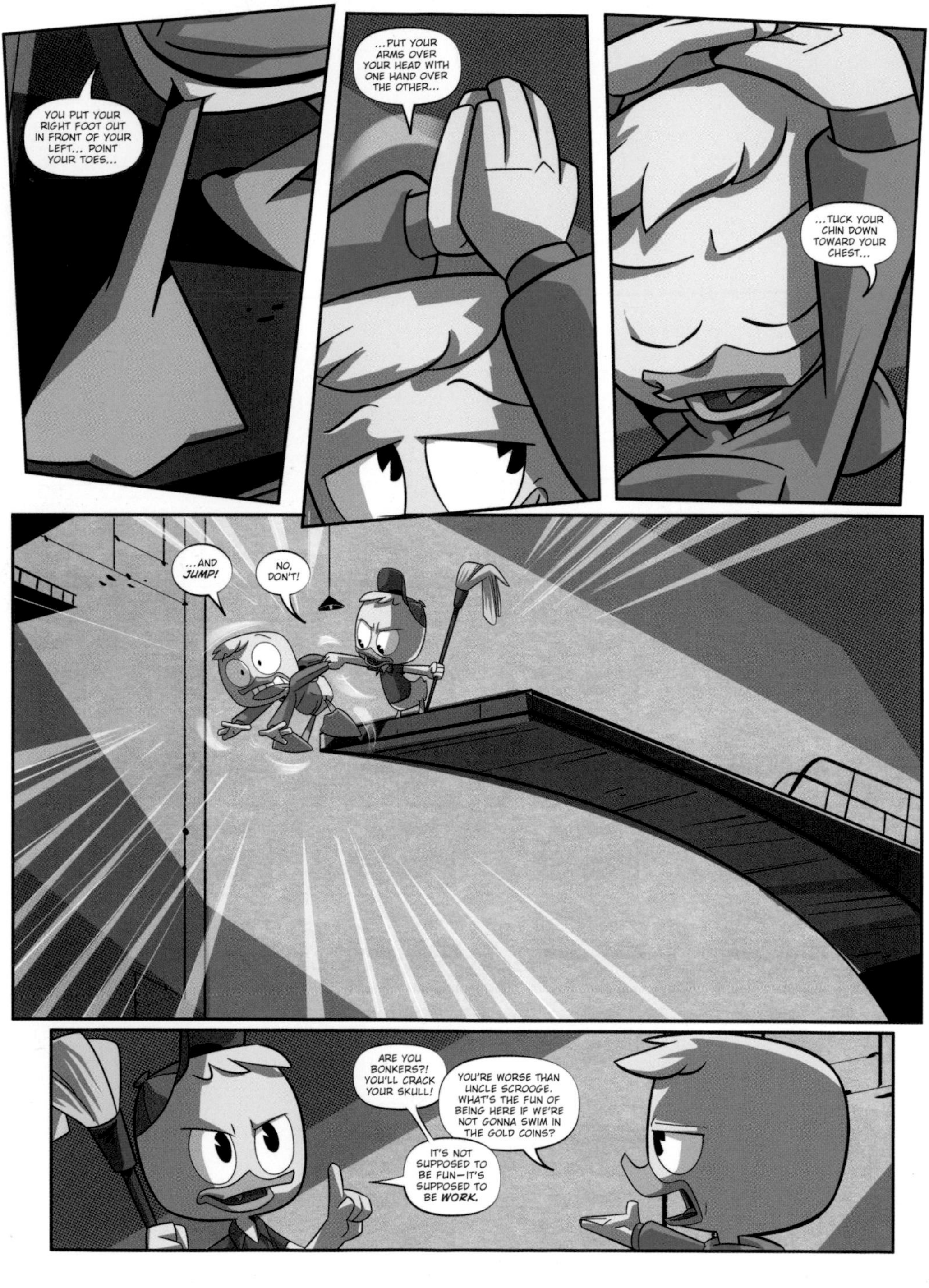
YOU PUT YOUR RIGHT FOOT OUT IN FRONT OF YOUR LEFT... POINT YOUR TOES...
...PUT YOUR ARMS OVER YOUR HEAD WITH ONE HAND OVER THE OTHER...
...TUCK YOUR CHIN DOWN TOWARD YOUR CHEST...
...AND JUMP!
NO, DON'T!
ARE YOU BONKERS?! YOU'LL CRACK YOUR SKULL!
YOU'RE WORSE THAN UNCLE SCROOGE. WHAT'S THE FUN OF BEING HERE IF WE'RE NOT GONNA SWIM IN THE GOLD COINS?
IT'S NOT SUPPOSED TO BE FUN—IT'S SUPPOSED TO BE WORK.

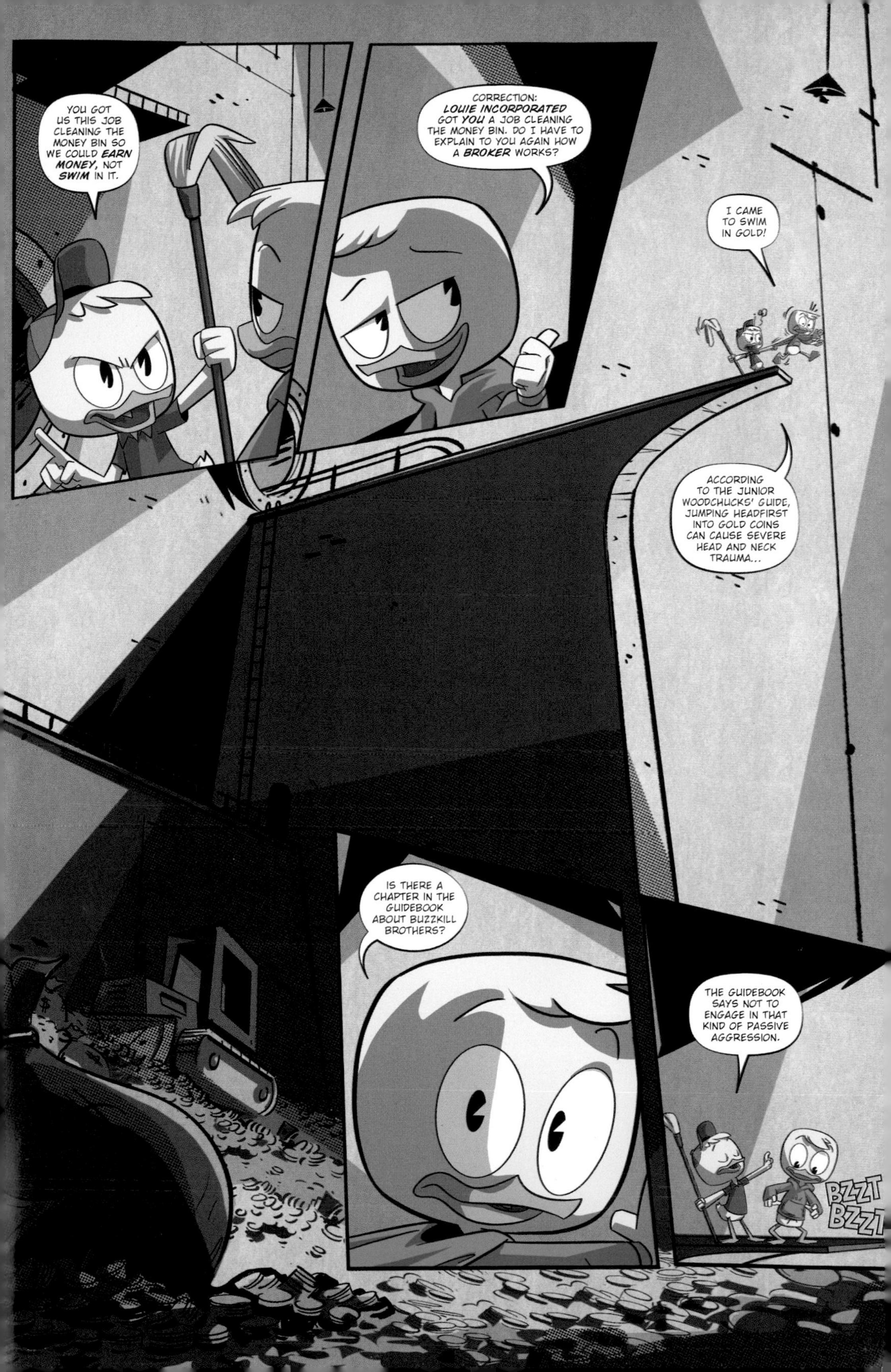
YOU GOT US THIS JOB CLEANING THE MONEY BIN SO WE COULD EARN MONEY, NOT SWIM IN IT.
CORRECTION: LOUIE INCORPORATED GOT YOU A JOB CLEANING THE MONEY BIN. DO I HAVE TO EXPLAIN TO YOU AGAIN HOW A BROKER WORKS?
I CAME TO SWIM IN GOLD!
ACCORDING TO THE JUNIOR WOODCHUCKS' GUIDE, JUMPING HEADFIRST INTO GOLD COINS CAN CAUSE SEVERE HEAD AND NECK TRAUMA...
IS THERE A CHAPTER IN THE GUIDEBOOK ABOUT BUZZKILL BROTHERS?
THE GUIDEBOOK SAYS NOT TO ENGAGE IN THAT KIND OF PASSIVE AGGRESSION.
BZZT BZZT

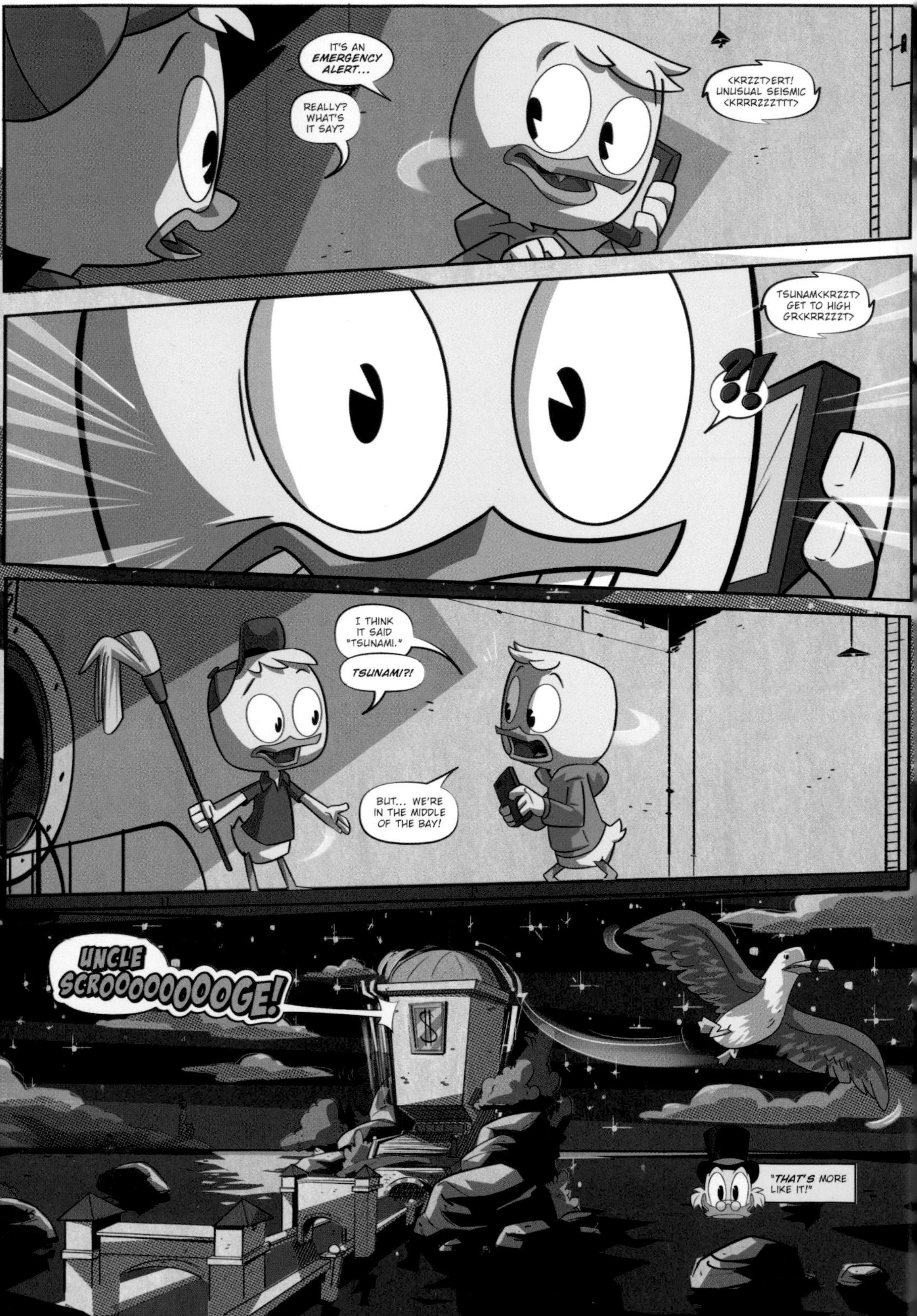
IT'S AN EMERGENCY ALERT...
REALLY? WHAT'S IT SAY?
<KRZZT>ERT! UNUSUAL SEISMIC <KRRRZZZTTT>
TSUNAM<KRZZT> GET TO HIGH GR<KRRZZZT>
?!
I THINK IT SAID "TSUNAMI."
TSUNAMI?!
BUT... WE'RE IN THE MIDDLE OF THE BAY!
UNCLE SCROOOOOOOOOGE!
"THAT'S MORE LIKE IT!"

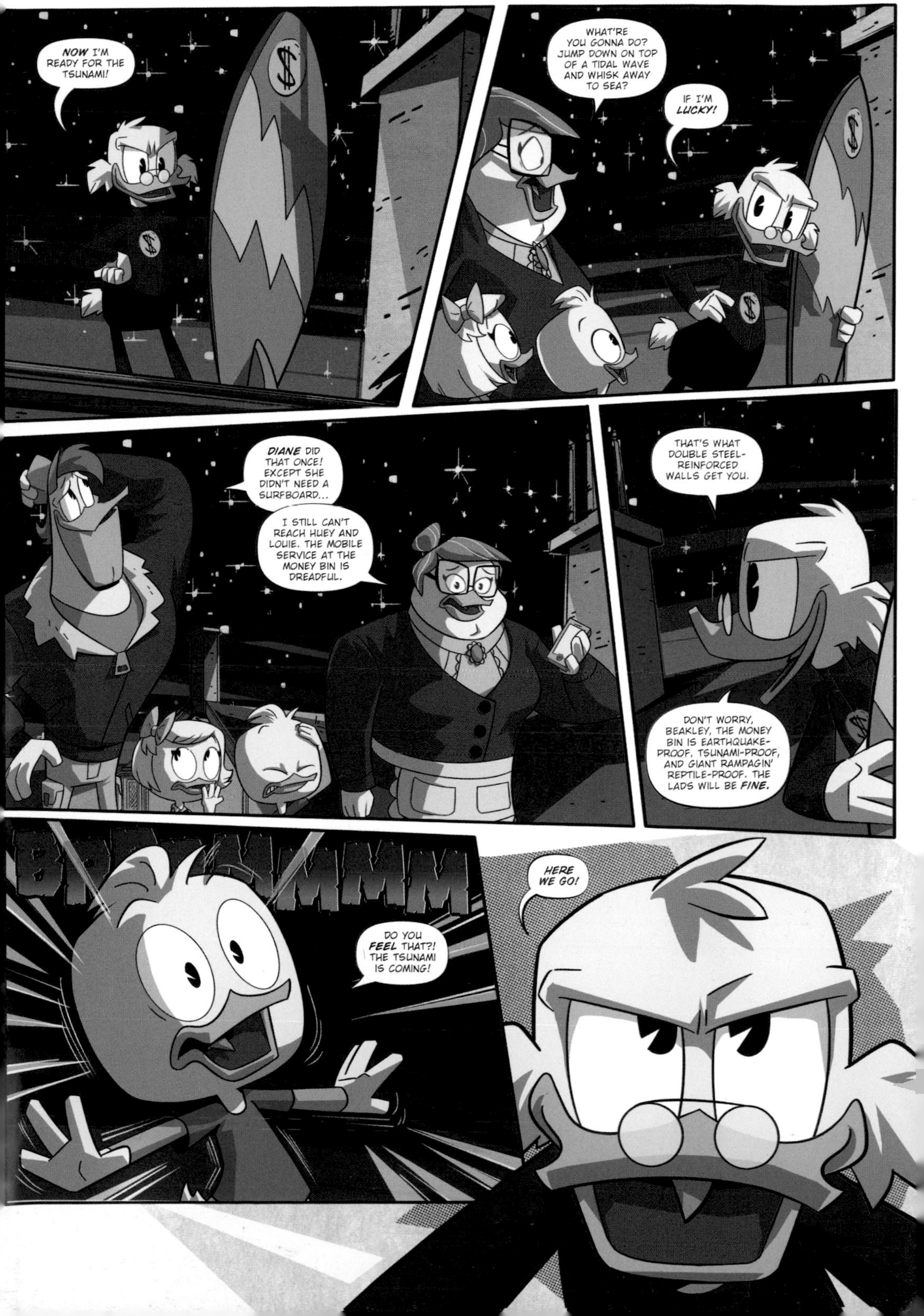
NOW I'M READY FOR THE TSUNAMI!
WHAT'RE YOU GONNA DO? JUMP DOWN ON TOP OF A TIDAL WAVE AND WHISK AWAY TO SEA?
IF I'M LUCKY!
DIANE DID THAT ONCE! EXCEPT SHE DIDN'T NEED A SURFBOARD...
I STILL CAN'T REACH HUEY AND LOUIE. THE MOBILE SERVICE AT THE MONEY BIN IS DREADFUL.
THAT'S WHAT DOUBLE STEEL-REINFORCED WALLS GET YOU.
DON'T WORRY, BEAKLEY, THE MONEY BIN IS EARTHQUAKE-PROOF, TSUNAMI-PROOF, AND GIANT RAMPAGIN' REPTILE-PROOF. THE LADS WILL BE FINE.
DO YOU FEEL THAT?! THE TSUNAMI IS COMING!
HERE WE GO!

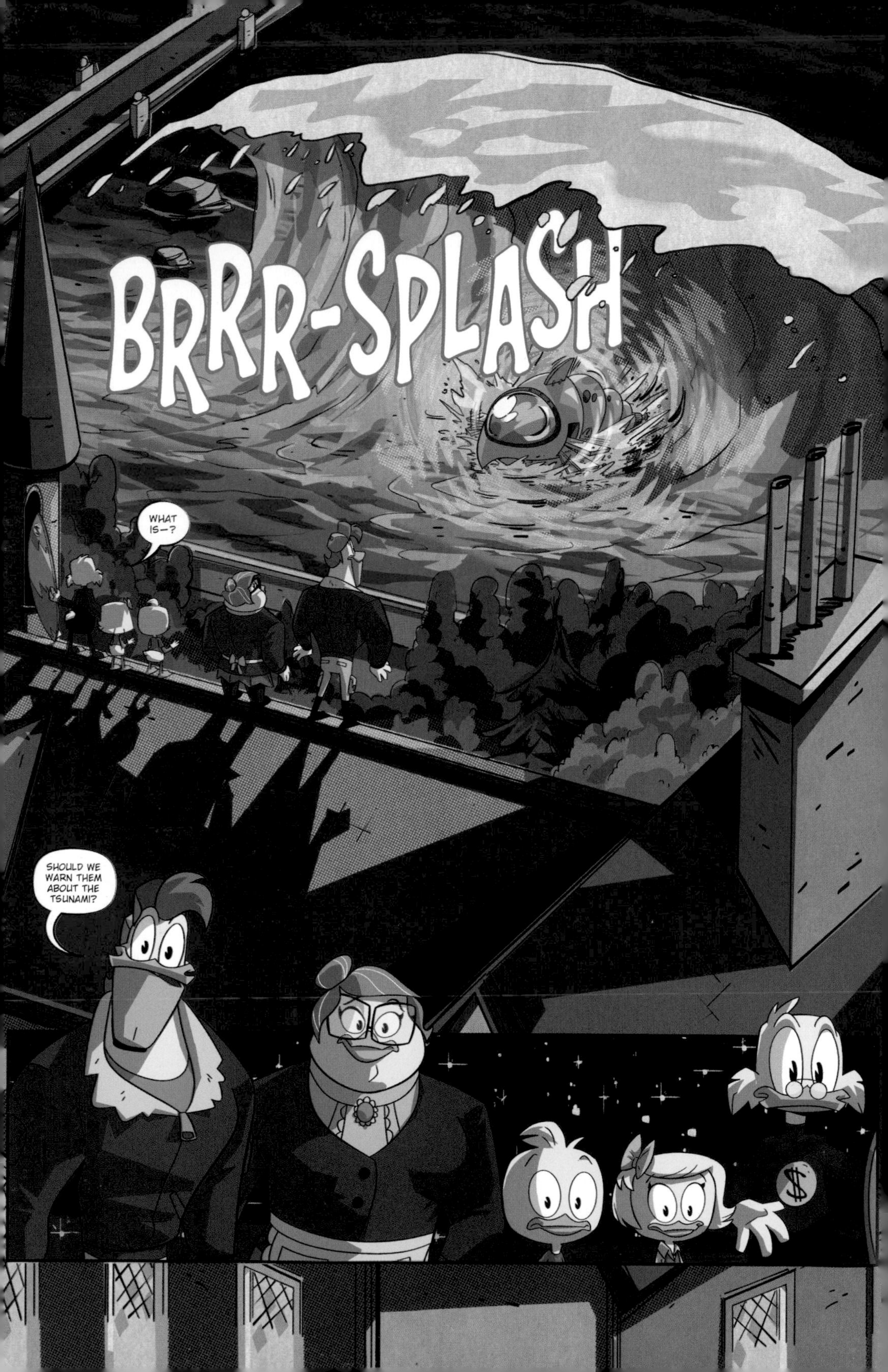
BRRR-SPLASH
WHAT IS—?
SHOULD WE WARN THEM ABOUT THE TSUNAMI?

THAT'S UNLIKE ANY SUBMARINE I'VE EVER SEEN.
WHERE ARE THEY FROM?
I DON'T KNOW WHO THEY ARE, BUT I KNOW WHAT THEY ARE...
...MONEY-GRUBBIN' HOOLIGANS FROM THE DEEP!
OBVIOUSLY SOMEONE'S ELABORATE SCHEME TO SNEAK UP ON MY TREASURE FROM BELOW! WE'VE GOT TO GET TO THE MONEY BIN!
AND GET HUEY AND LOUIE OUT OF THERE!
LAUNCHPAD, GET THE CAR!
I HAVE AN IDEA: I'LL GET THE CAR!

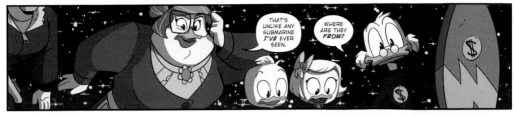

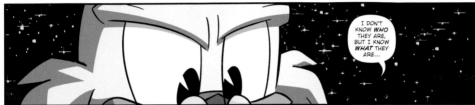

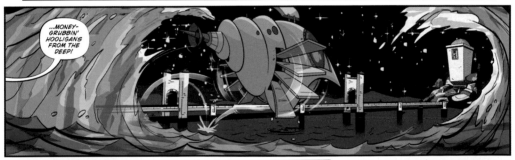

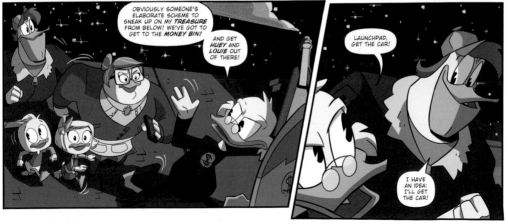

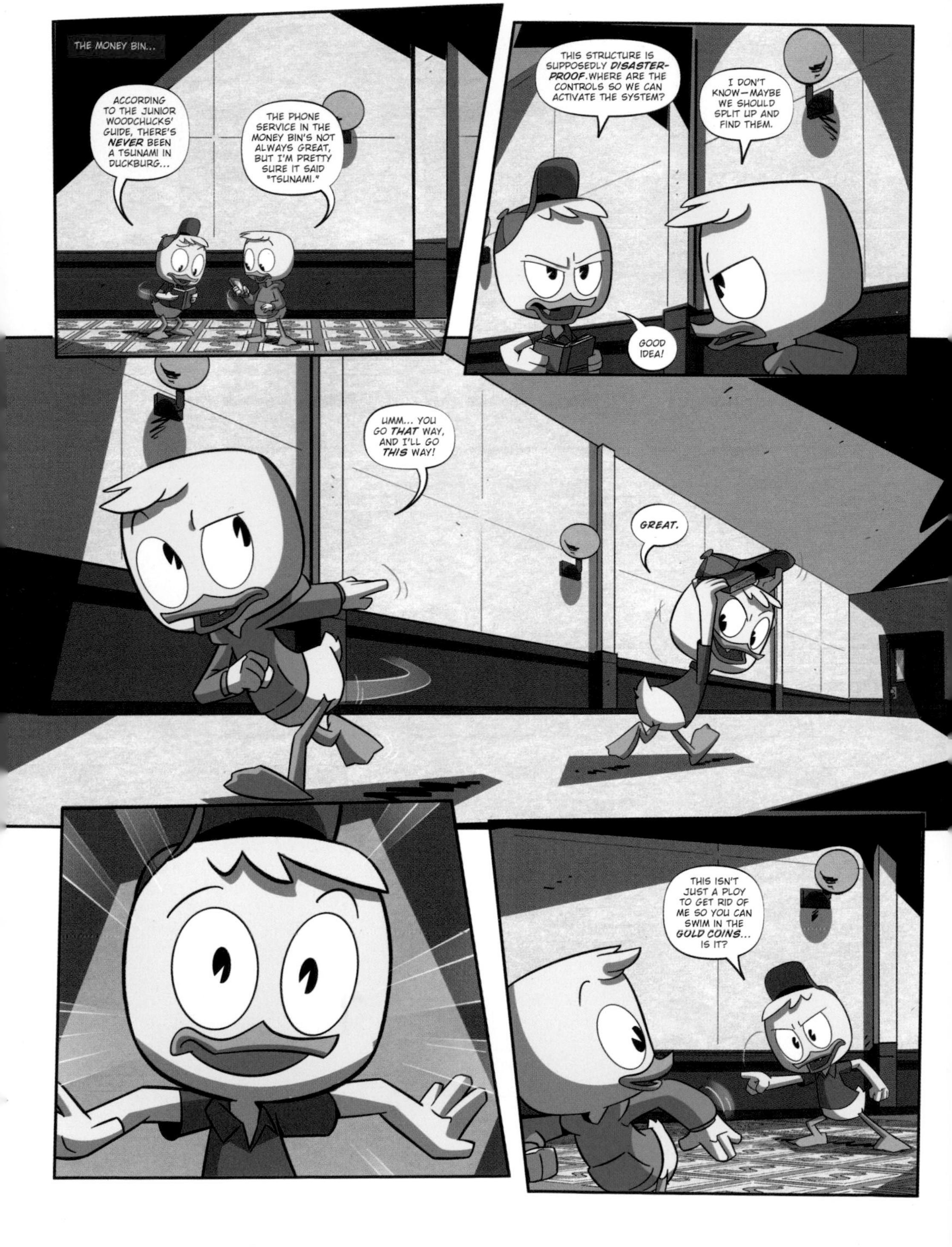
THE MONEY BIN...
ACCORDING TO THE JUNIOR WOODCHUCKS' GUIDE, THERE'S NEVER BEEN A TSUNAMI IN DUCKBURG...
THE PHONE SERVICE IN THE MONEY BIN'S NOT ALWAYS GREAT, BUT I'M PRETTY SURE IT SAID "TSUNAMI."
THIS STRUCTURE IS SUPPOSEDLY DISASTER-PROOF. WHERE ARE THE CONTROLS SO WE CAN ACTIVATE THE SYSTEM?
I DON'T KNOW—MAYBE WE SHOULD SPLIT UP AND FIND THEM.
GOOD IDEA!
UMM... YOU GO THAT WAY, AND I'LL GO THIS WAY!
GREAT.
THIS ISN'T JUST A PLOY TO GET RID OF ME SO YOU CAN SWIM IN THE GOLD COINS... IS IT?

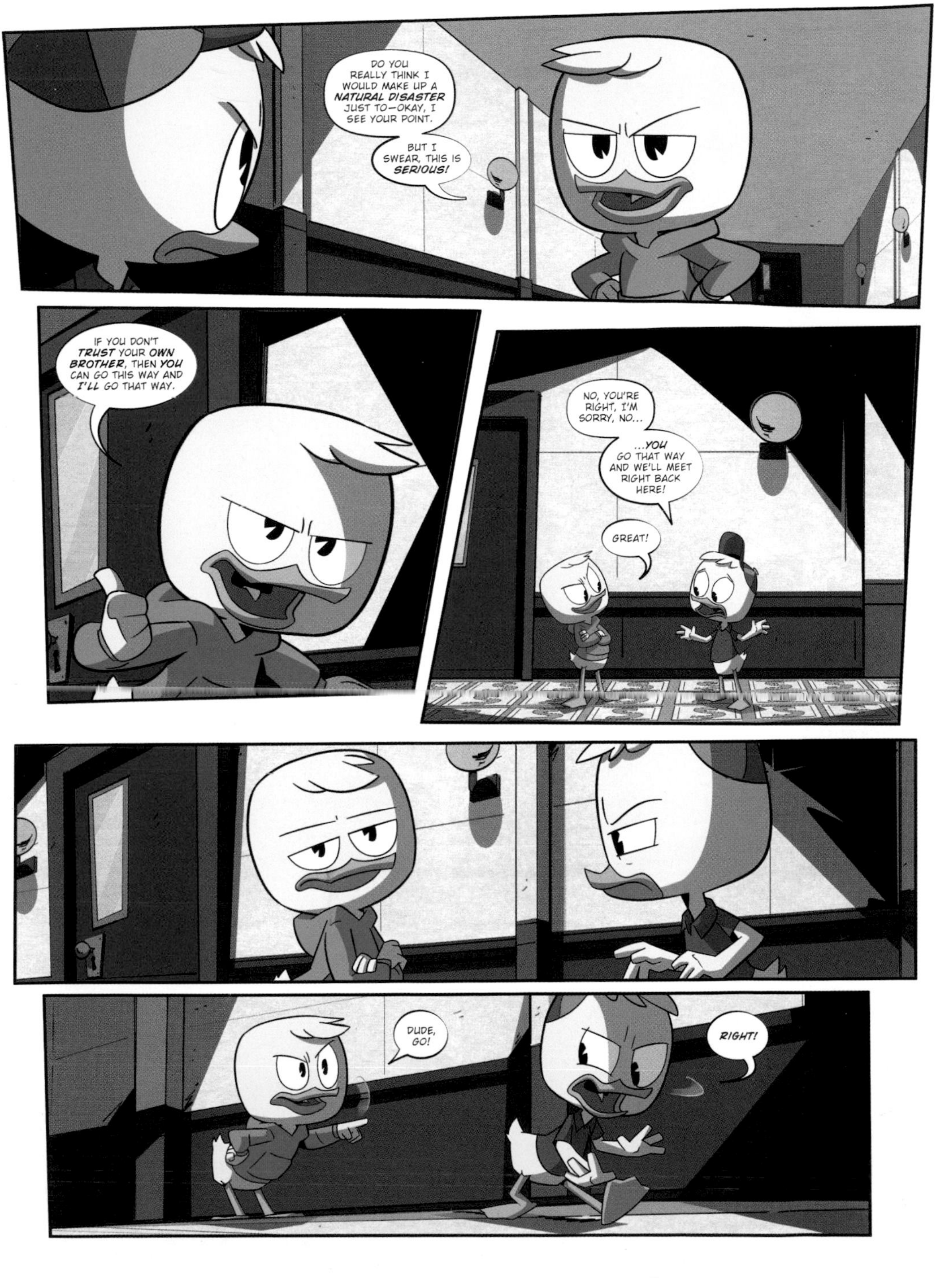

DO YOU REALLY THINK I WOULD MAKE UP A NATURAL DISASTER JUST TO—OKAY, I SEE YOUR POINT.
BUT I SWEAR, THIS IS SERIOUS!
IF YOU DON'T TRUST YOUR OWN BROTHER, THEN YOU CAN GO THIS WAY AND I'LL GO THAT WAY.
NO, YOU'RE RIGHT, I'M SORRY, NO...
...YOU GO THAT WAY AND WE'LL MEET RIGHT BACK HERE!
GREAT!
DUDE, GO!
RIGHT!

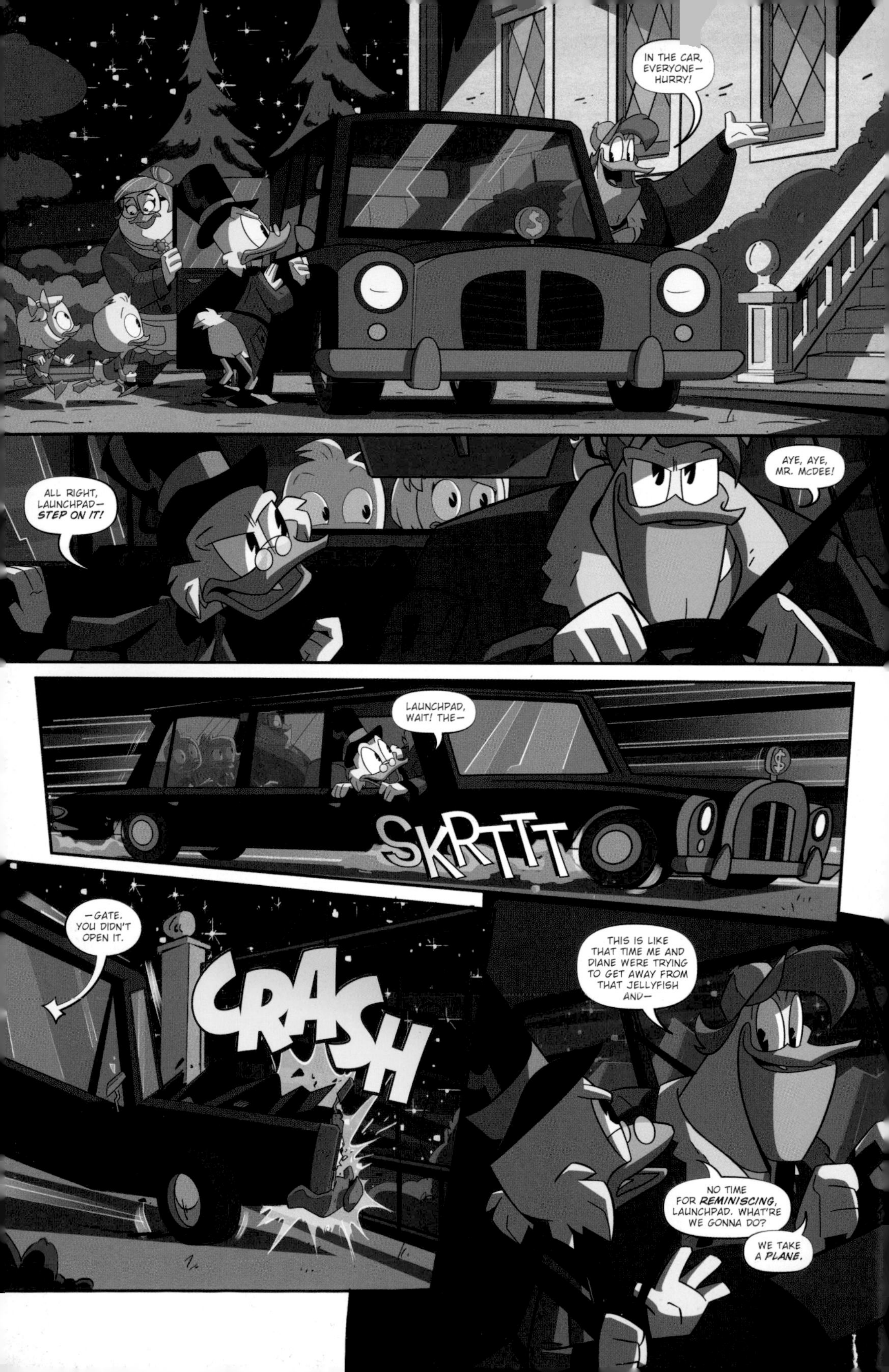
IN THE CAR, EVERYONE— HURRY!
ALL RIGHT, LAUNCHPAD— STEP ON IT!
AYE, AYE, MR. MCDEE!
LAUNCHPAD, WAIT! THE—
SKRTTT
—GATE. YOU DIDN'T OPEN IT.
CRASH
THIS IS LIKE THAT TIME ME AND DIANE WERE TRYING TO GET AWAY FROM THAT JELLYFISH AND—
NO TIME FOR REMINISCING, LAUNCHPAD. WHAT'RE WE GONNA DO?
WE TAKE A PLANE.

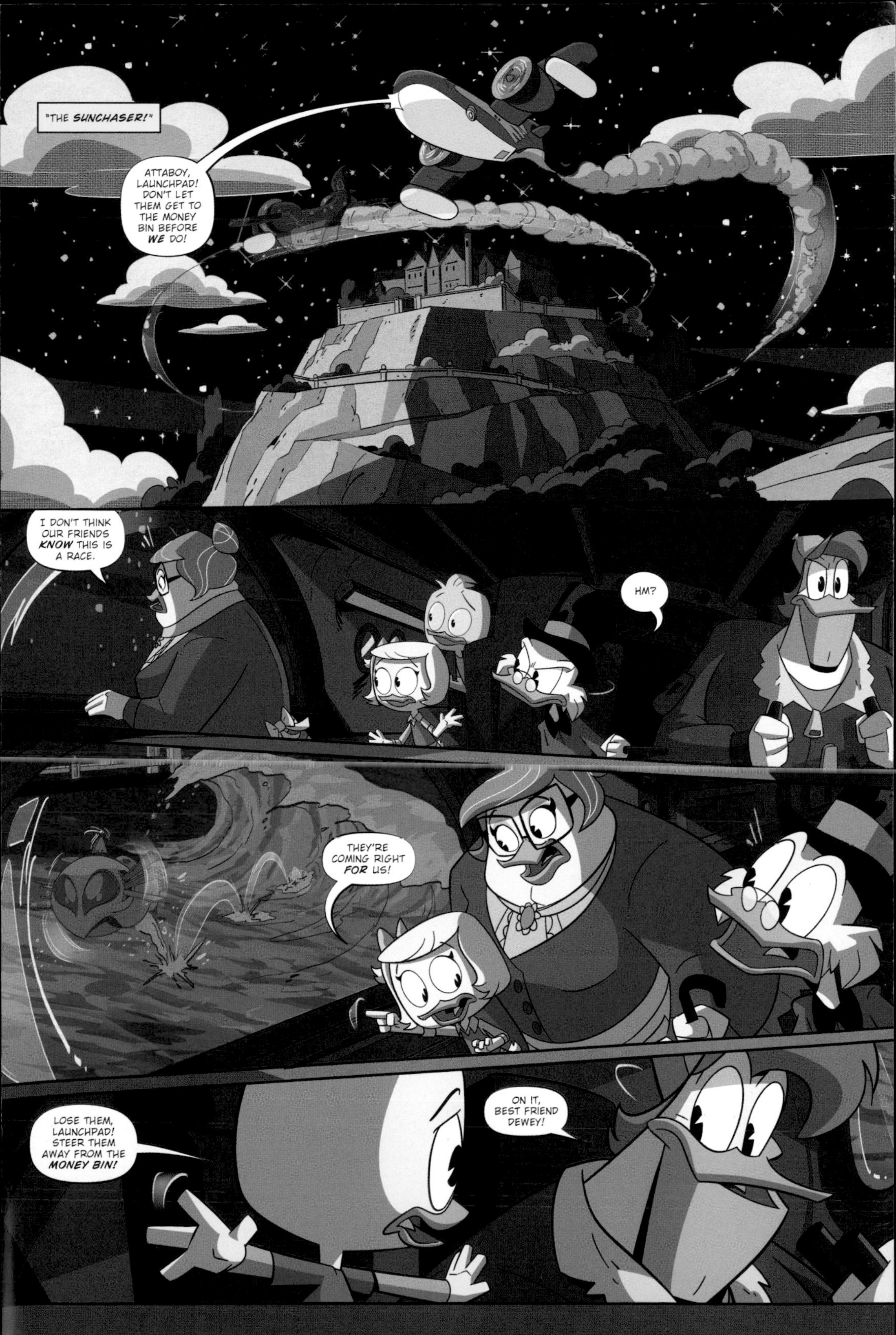
"THE SUNCHASER!"
ATTABOY, LAUNCHPAD! DON'T LET THEM GET TO THE MONEY BIN BEFORE WE DO!
I DON'T THINK OUR FRIENDS KNOW THIS IS A RACE.
HM?
THEY'RE COMING RIGHT FOR US!
LOSE THEM, LAUNCHPAD! STEER THEM AWAY FROM THE MONEY BIN!
ON IT, BEST FRIEND DEWEY!

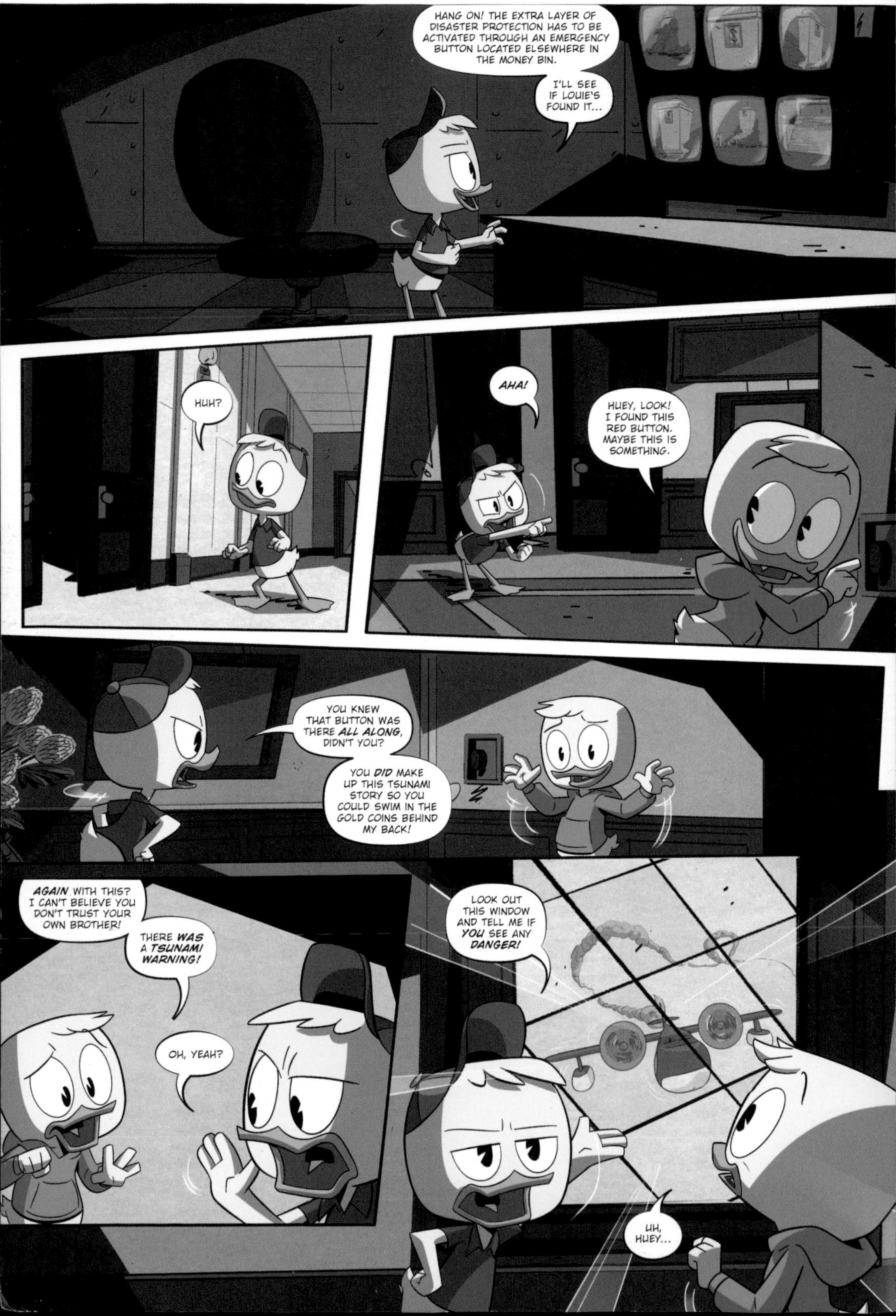
HANG ON! THE EXTRA LAYER OF DISASTER PROTECTION HAS TO BE ACTIVATED THROUGH AN EMERGENCY BUTTON LOCATED ELSEWHERE IN THE MONEY BIN.
I'LL SEE IF LOUIE'S FOUND IT...
HUH?
AHA!
HUEY, LOOK! I FOUND THIS RED BUTTON. MAYBE THIS IS SOMETHING.
YOU KNEW THAT BUTTON WAS THERE ALL ALONG, DIDN'T YOU?
YOU DID MAKE UP THIS TSUNAMI STORY SO YOU COULD SWIM IN THE GOLD COINS BEHIND MY BACK!
AGAIN WITH THIS? I CAN'T BELIEVE YOU DON'T TRUST YOUR OWN BROTHER!
THERE WAS A TSUNAMI WARNING!
OH, YEAH?
LOOK OUT THIS WINDOW AND TELL ME IF YOU SEE ANY DANGER!
UH, HUEY...

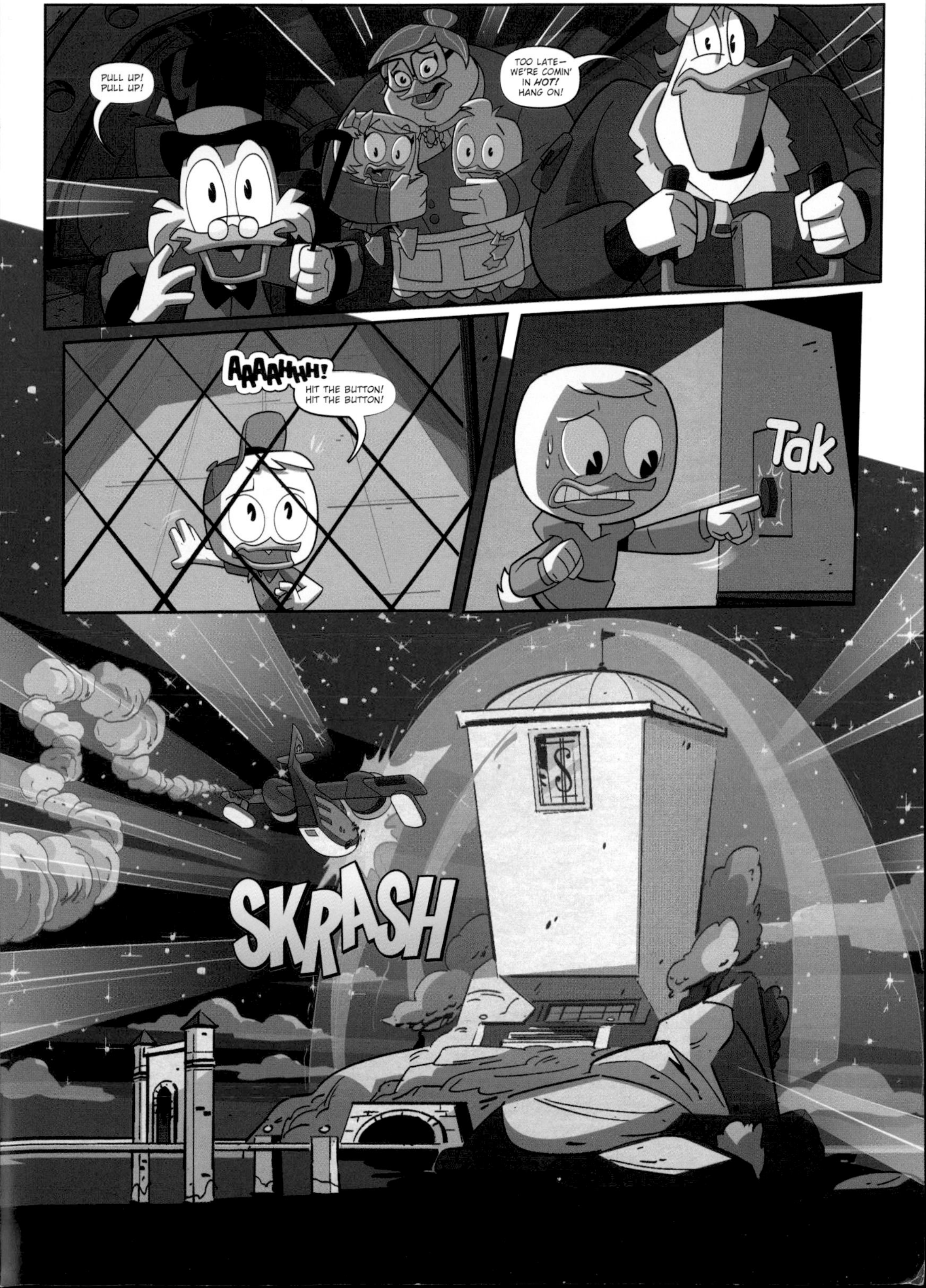
PULL UP! PULL UP!
TOO LATE— WE'RE COMIN' IN HOT! HANG ON!
AAAAHHH!
HIT THE BUTTON! HIT THE BUTTON!
Tak
SKRASH

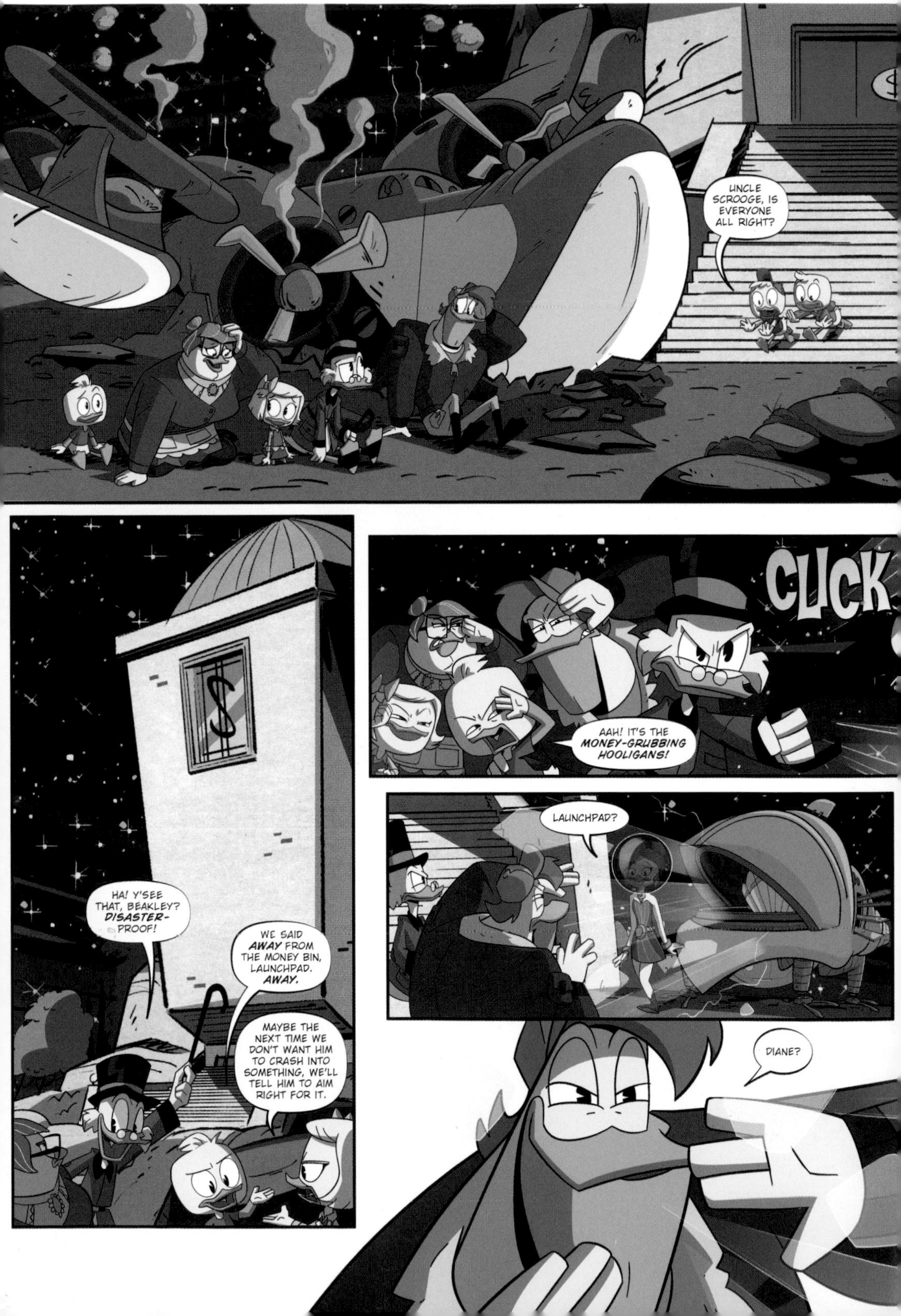

UNCLE SCROOGE, IS EVERYONE ALL RIGHT?
HA! Y'SEE THAT, BEAKLEY? DISASTER-PROOF!
WE SAID AWAY FROM THE MONEY BIN, LAUNCHPAD. AWAY.
MAYBE THE NEXT TIME WE DON'T WANT HIM TO CRASH INTO SOMETHING, WE'LL TELL HIM TO AIM RIGHT FOR IT.
CLICK
AAH! IT'S THE MONEY-GRUBBING HOOLIGANS!
LAUNCHPAD?
DIANE?

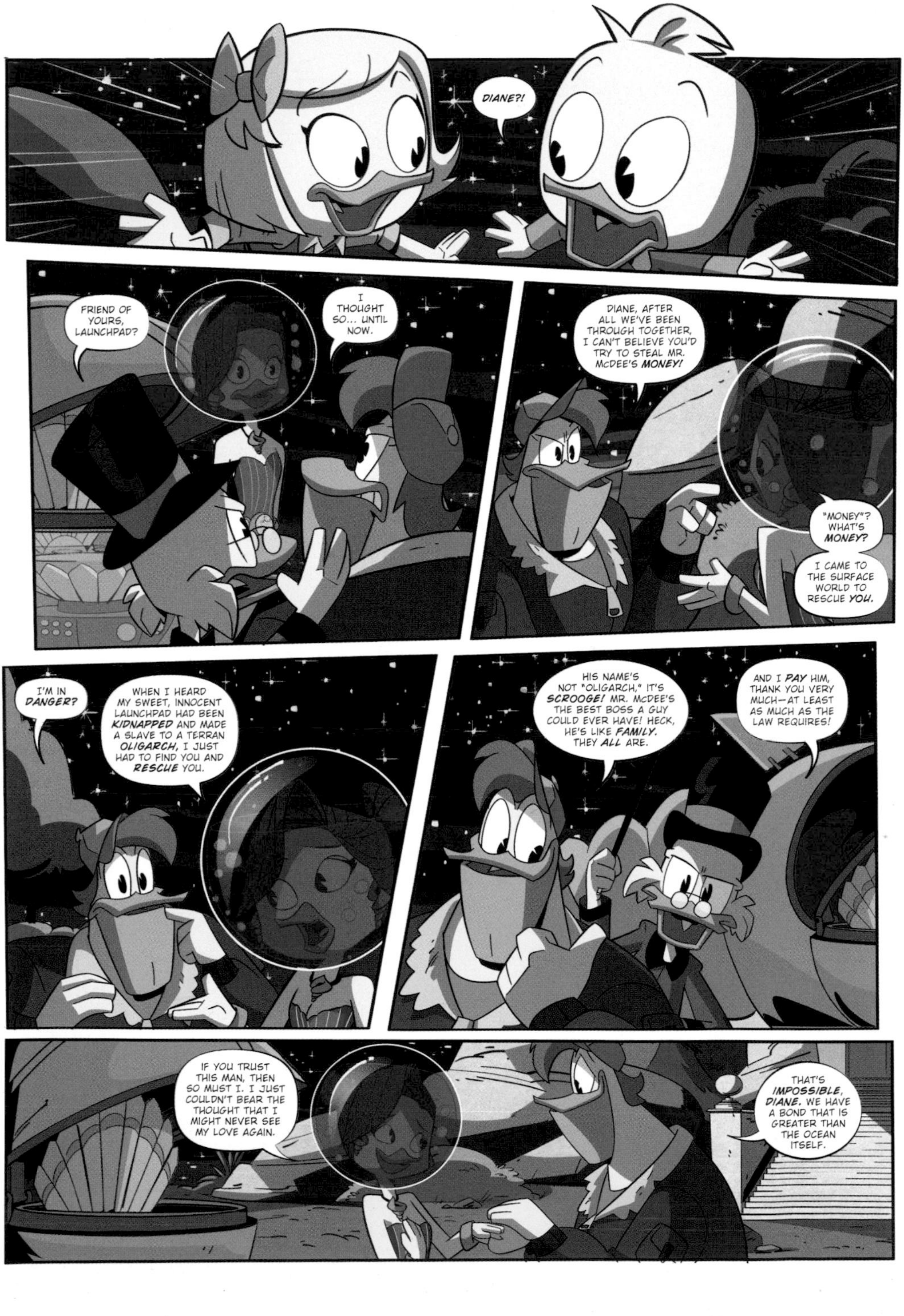
DIANE?!
FRIEND OF YOURS, LAUNCHPAD?
I THOUGHT SO... UNTIL NOW.
DIANE, AFTER ALL WE'VE BEEN THROUGH TOGETHER, I CAN'T BELIEVE YOU'D TRY TO STEAL MR. McDEE'S MONEY!
"MONEY"? WHAT'S MONEY?
I CAME TO THE SURFACE WORLD TO RESCUE YOU.
I'M IN DANGER?
WHEN I HEARD MY SWEET, INNOCENT LAUNCHPAD HAD BEEN KIDNAPPED AND MADE A SLAVE TO A TERRAN OLIGARCH, I JUST HAD TO FIND YOU AND RESCUE YOU.
HIS NAME'S NOT "OLIGARCH," IT'S SCROOGE! MR. McDEE'S THE BEST BOSS A GUY COULD EVER HAVE! HECK, HE'S LIKE FAMILY. THEY ALL ARE.
AND I PAY HIM, THANK YOU VERY MUCH—AT LEAST AS MUCH AS THE LAW REQUIRES!
IF YOU TRUST THIS MAN, THEN SO MUST I. I JUST COULDN'T BEAR THE THOUGHT THAT I MIGHT NEVER SEE MY LOVE AGAIN.
THAT'S IMPOSSIBLE, DIANE. WE HAVE A BOND THAT IS GREATER THAN THE OCEAN ITSELF.

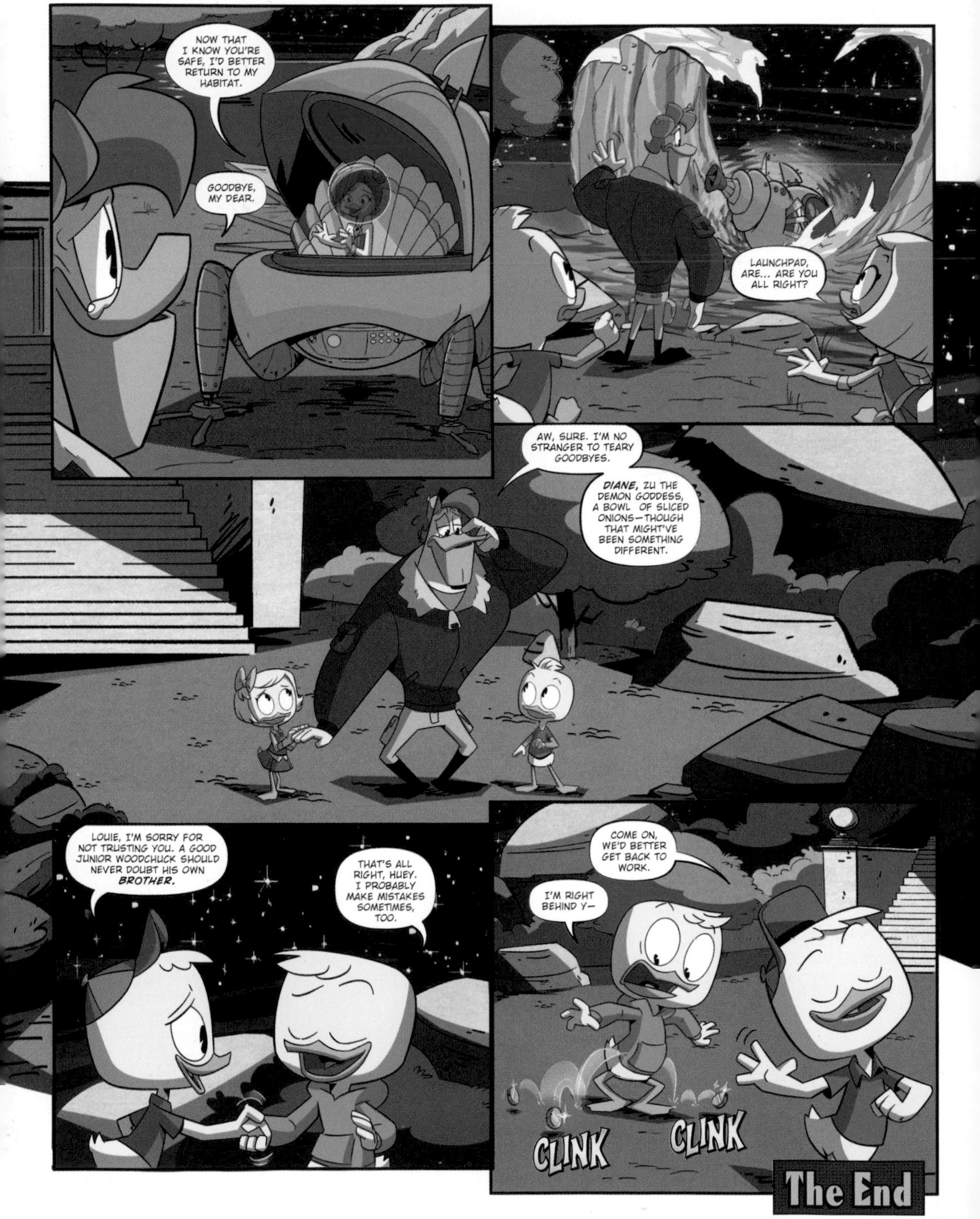
NOW THAT I KNOW YOU'RE SAFE, I'D BETTER RETURN TO MY HABITAT.
GOODBYE, MY DEAR.
LAUNCHPAD, ARE... ARE YOU ALL RIGHT?
AW, SURE. I'M NO STRANGER TO TEARY GOODBYES.
DIANE, ZU THE DEMON GODDESS, A BOWL OF SLICED ONIONS—THOUGH THAT MIGHT'VE BEEN SOMETHING DIFFERENT.
LOUIE, I'M SORRY FOR NOT TRUSTING YOU. A GOOD JUNIOR WOODCHUCK SHOULD NEVER DOUBT HIS OWN BROTHER.
THAT'S ALL RIGHT, HUEY. I PROBABLY MAKE MISTAKES SOMETIMES, TOO.
COME ON, WE'D BETTER GET BACK TO WORK.
I'M RIGHT BEHIND Y—
CLINK
CLINK
The End

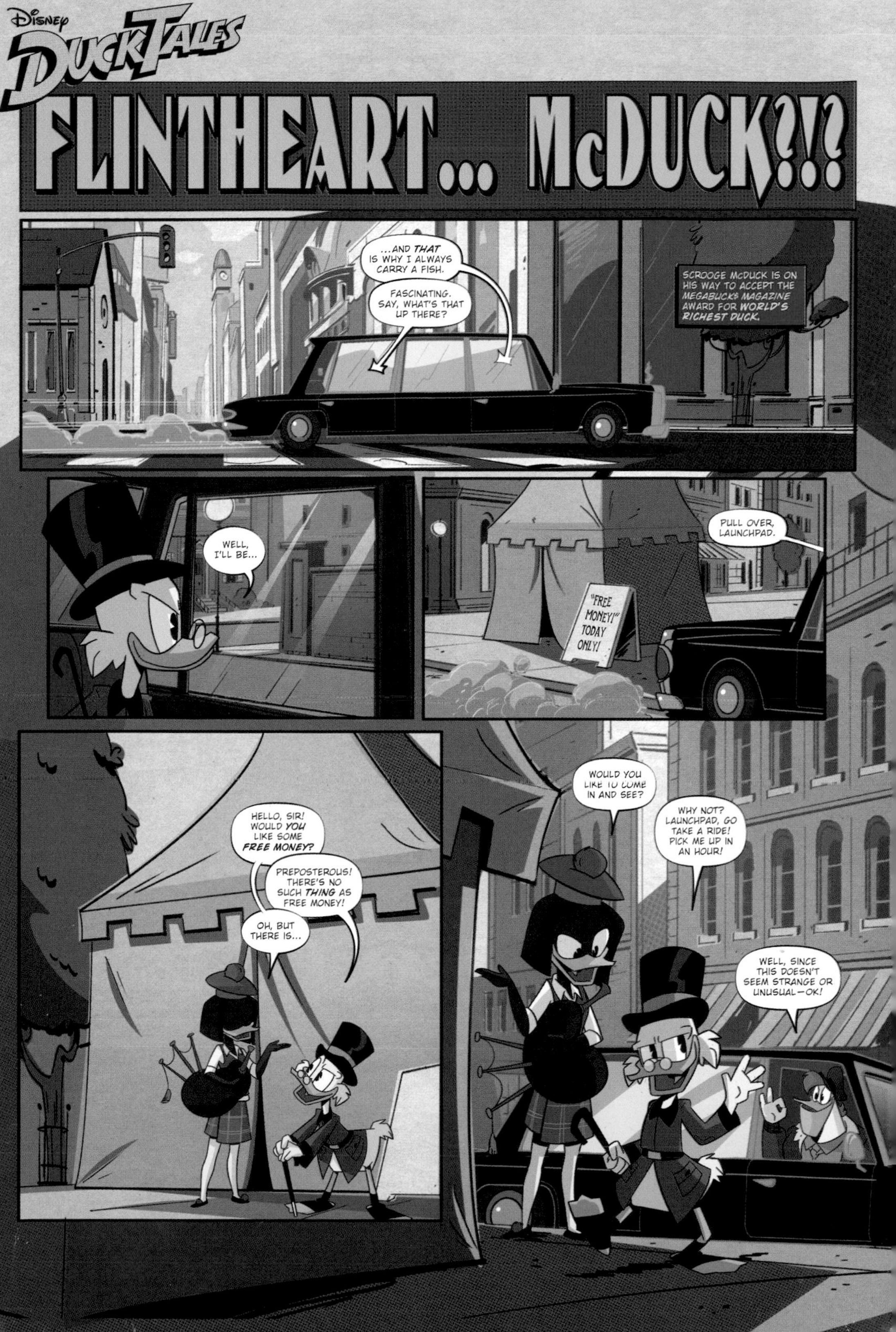
DISNEY
DUCKTALES
FLINTHEART... McDUCK?!?
...AND THAT IS WHY I ALWAYS CARRY A FISH.
FASCINATING. SAY, WHAT'S THAT UP THERE?
SCROOGE McDUCK IS ON HIS WAY TO ACCEPT THE MEGABUCK$ MAGAZINE AWARD FOR WORLD'S RICHEST DUCK.
WELL, I'LL BE...
PULL OVER, LAUNCHPAD.
"FREE MONEY!" TODAY ONLY!
HELLO, SIR! WOULD YOU LIKE SOME FREE MONEY?
PREPOSTEROUS! THERE'S NO SUCH THING AS FREE MONEY!
OH, BUT THERE IS...
WOULD YOU LIKE TO COME IN AND SEE?
WHY NOT? LAUNCHPAD, GO TAKE A RIDE! PICK ME UP IN AN HOUR!
WELL, SINCE THIS DOESN'T SEEM STRANGE OR UNUSUAL—OK!

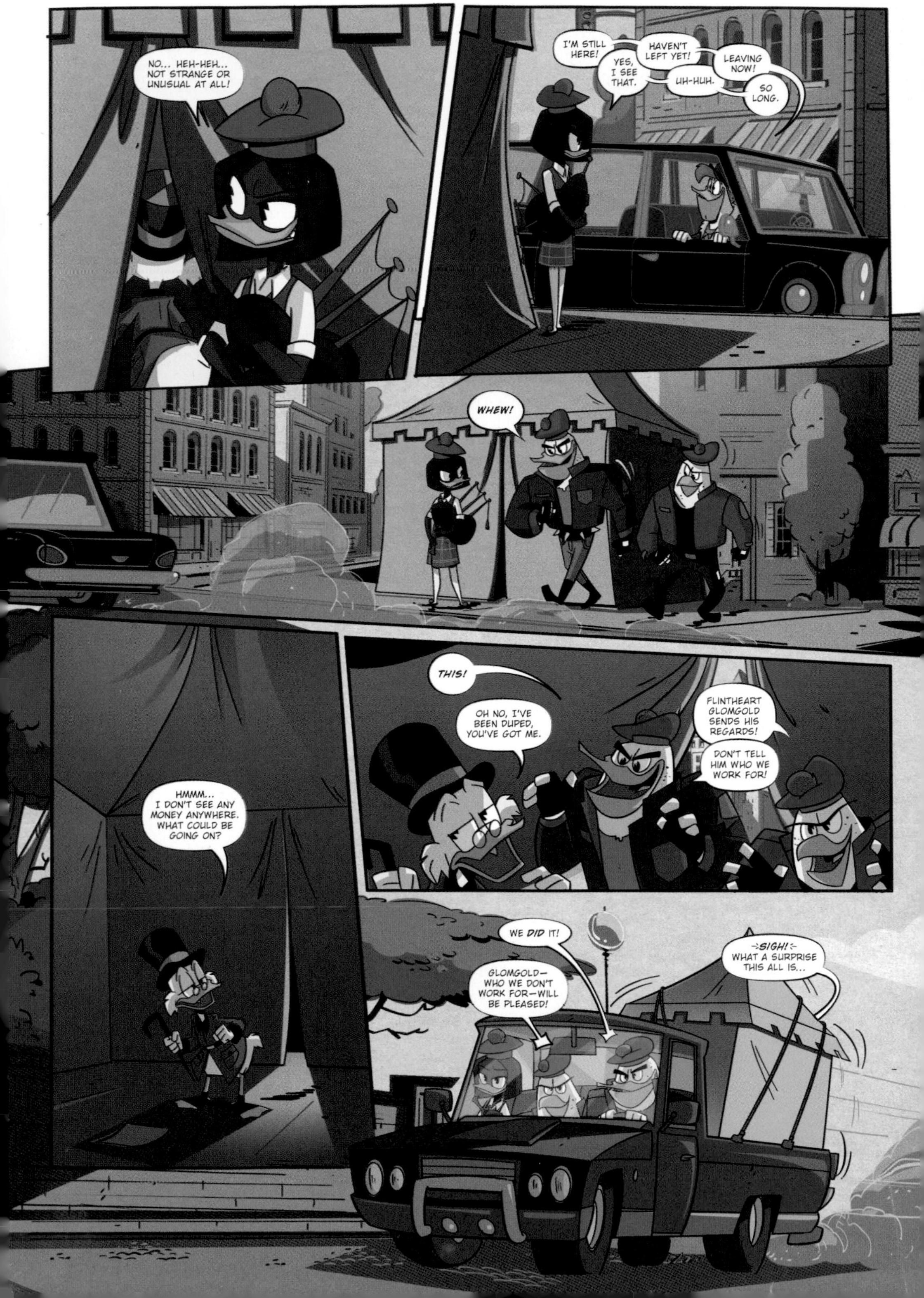
NO... HEH-HEH... NOT STRANGE OR UNUSUAL AT ALL!
I'M STILL HERE!
HAVEN'T LEFT YET!
YES, I SEE THAT.
UH-HUH.
LEAVING NOW!
SO LONG.
WHEW!
HMMM... I DON'T SEE ANY MONEY ANYWHERE. WHAT COULD BE GOING ON?
THIS!
OH NO, I'VE BEEN DUPED, YOU'VE GOT ME.
FLINTHEART GLOMGOLD SENDS HIS REGARDS!
DON'T TELL HIM WHO WE WORK FOR!
WE DID IT!
GLOMGOLD— WHO WE DON'T WORK FOR—WILL BE PLEASED!
SIGH! WHAT A SURPRISE THIS ALL IS...

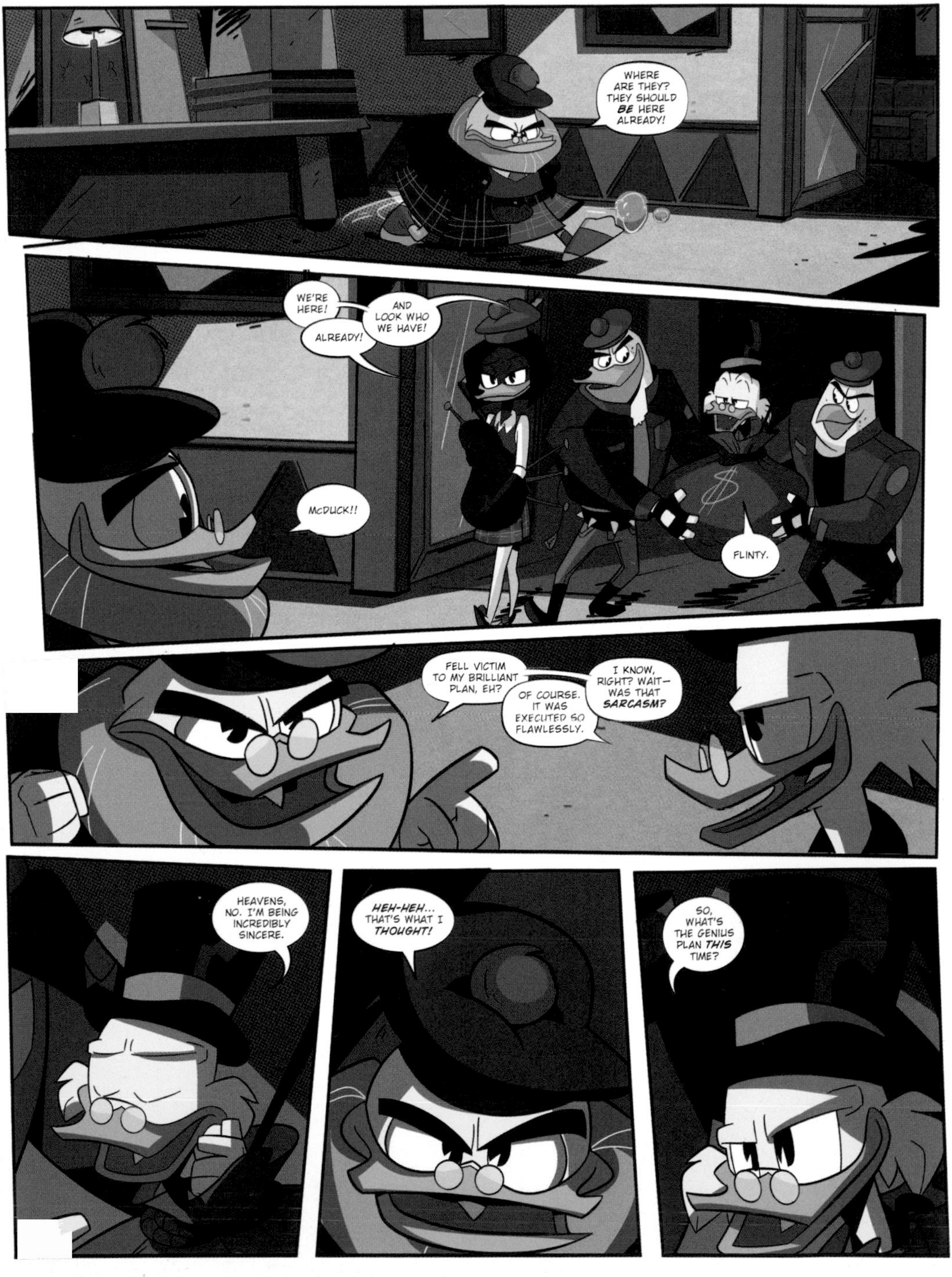
WHERE ARE THEY? THEY SHOULD BE HERE ALREADY!
WE'RE HERE!
ALREADY!
AND LOOK WHO WE HAVE!
McDUCK!!
FLINTY.
FELL VICTIM TO MY BRILLIANT PLAN, EH?
OF COURSE. IT WAS EXECUTED SO FLAWLESSLY.
I KNOW, RIGHT? WAIT— WAS THAT SARCASM?
HEAVENS, NO. I'M BEING INCREDIBLY SINCERE.
HEH-HEH... THAT'S WHAT I THOUGHT!
SO, WHAT'S THE GENIUS PLAN THIS TIME?

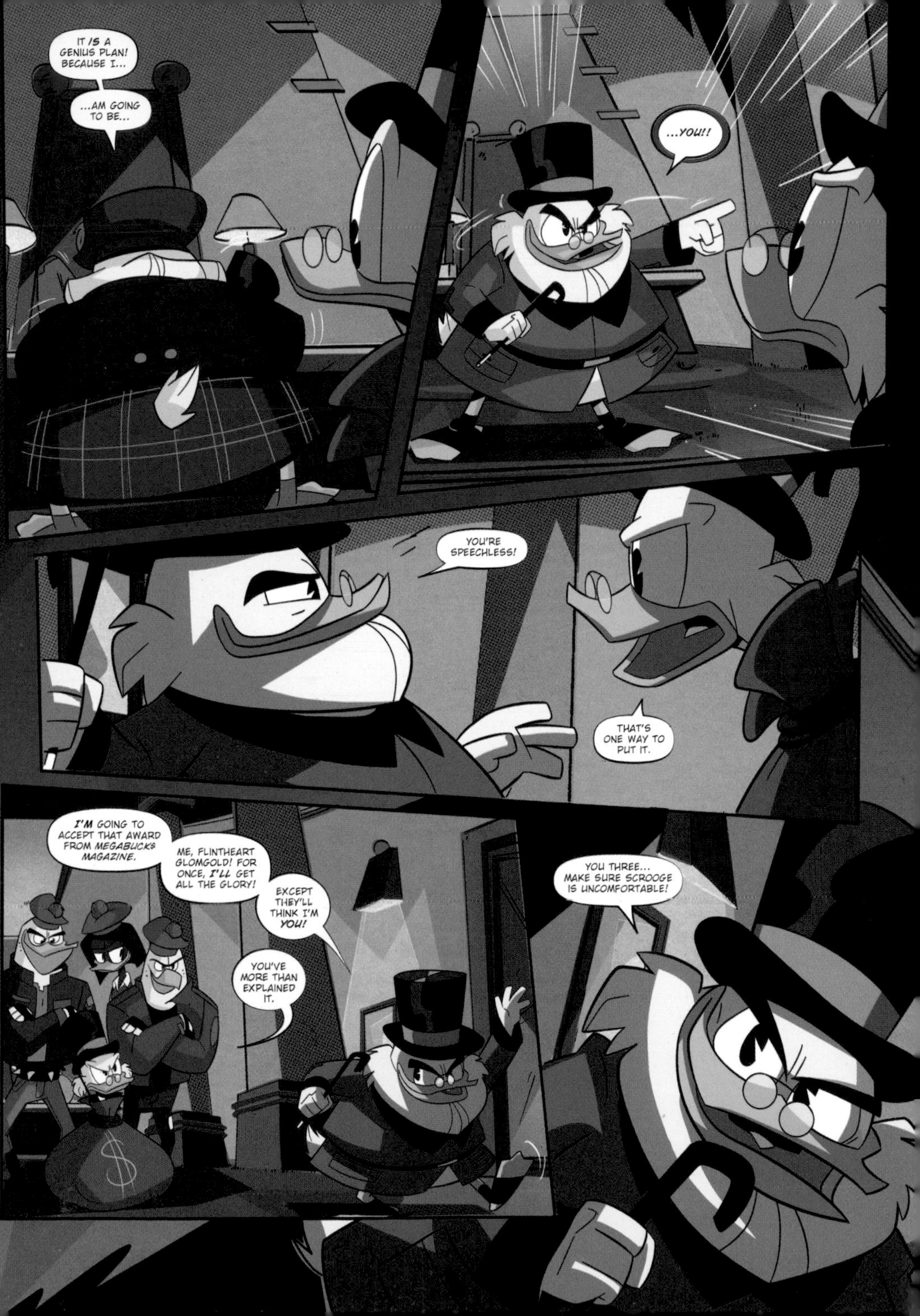

IT *IS* A GENIUS PLAN! BECAUSE I...
...AM GOING TO BE...
...*YOU!!*
YOU'RE SPEECHLESS!
THAT'S ONE WAY TO PUT IT.
I'M GOING TO ACCEPT THAT AWARD FROM *MEGABUCK$ MAGAZINE.*
ME, FLINTHEART GLOMGOLD! FOR ONCE, *I'LL* GET ALL THE GLORY!
EXCEPT THEY'LL THINK I'M *YOU!*
YOU'VE MORE THAN EXPLAINED IT.
YOU THREE... MAKE SURE SCROOGE IS UNCOMFORTABLE!

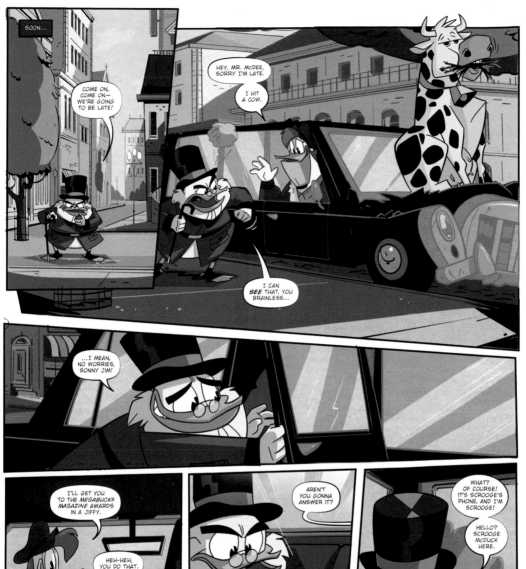

SOON...

COME ON, COME ON— WE'RE GOING TO BE LATE!

HEY, MR. McDEE, SORRY I'M LATE.

I HIT A COW.

I CAN *SEE* THAT, YOU BRAINLESS...

...I MEAN, NO WORRIES, SONNY JIM!

I'LL GET YOU TO THE *MEGABUCKS MAGAZINE AWARDS* IN A JIFFY.

HEH-HEH, YOU DO THAT.

AREN'T YOU GONNA ANSWER IT?

RRRING RRRING

WHAT? OF COURSE! IT'S SCROOGE'S PHONE, AND I'M SCROOGE!

HELLO? SCROOGE McDUCK HERE.

IT'S BRADFORD BUZZARD FROM THE BOARD. WE NEED TO TALK ABOUT THE *BUDGET.*

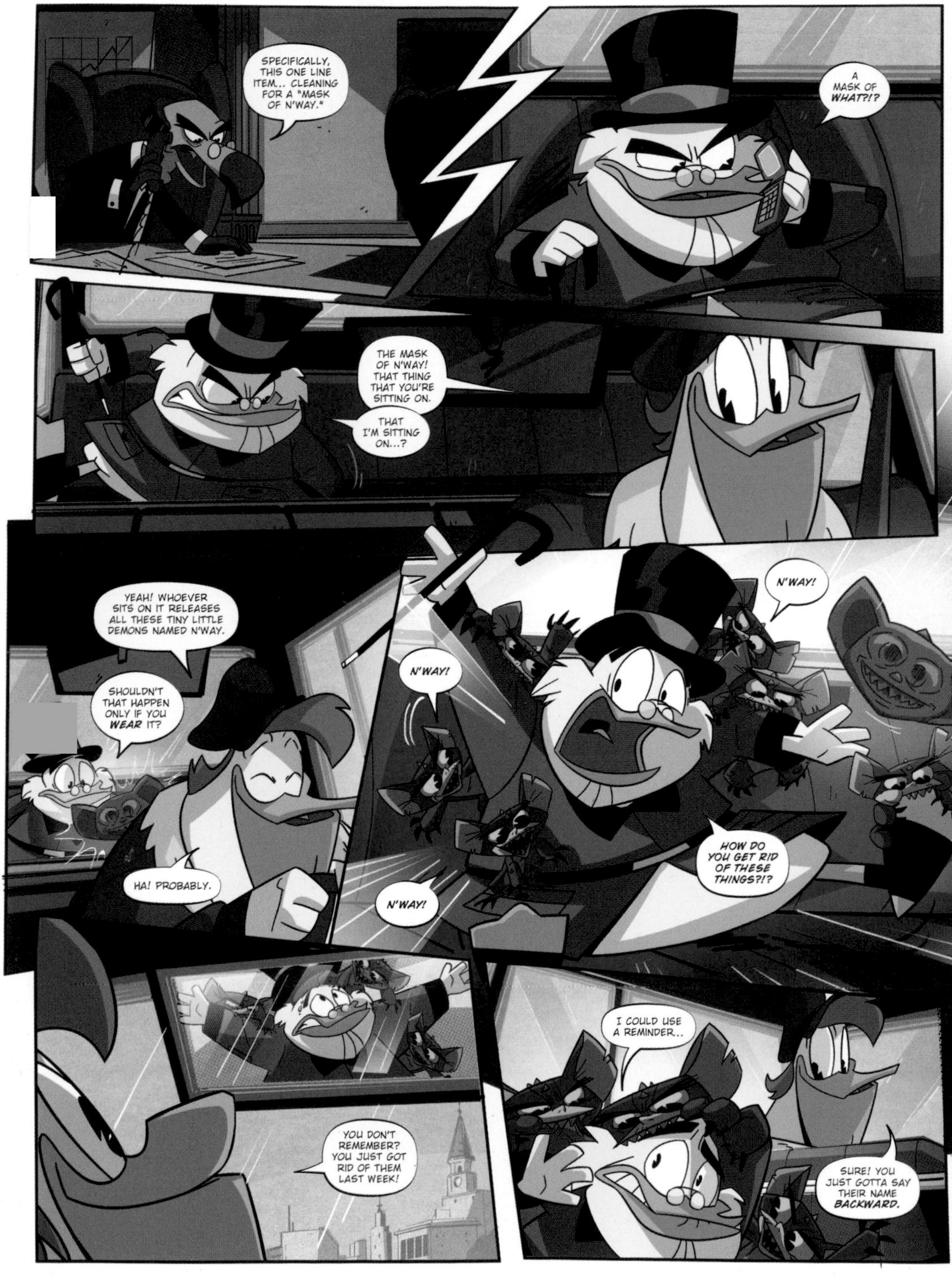

SPECIFICALLY, THIS ONE LINE ITEM... CLEANING FOR A "MASK OF N'WAY."
A MASK OF WHAT?!?
THE MASK OF N'WAY! THAT THING THAT YOU'RE SITTING ON.
THAT I'M SITTING ON...?
YEAH! WHOEVER SITS ON IT RELEASES ALL THESE TINY LITTLE DEMONS NAMED N'WAY.
SHOULDN'T THAT HAPPEN ONLY IF YOU WEAR IT?
HA! PROBABLY.
N'WAY!
N'WAY!
HOW DO YOU GET RID OF THESE THINGS?!?
N'WAY!
YOU DON'T REMEMBER? YOU JUST GOT RID OF THEM LAST WEEK!
I COULD USE A REMINDER...
SURE! YOU JUST GOTTA SAY THEIR NAME BACKWARD.

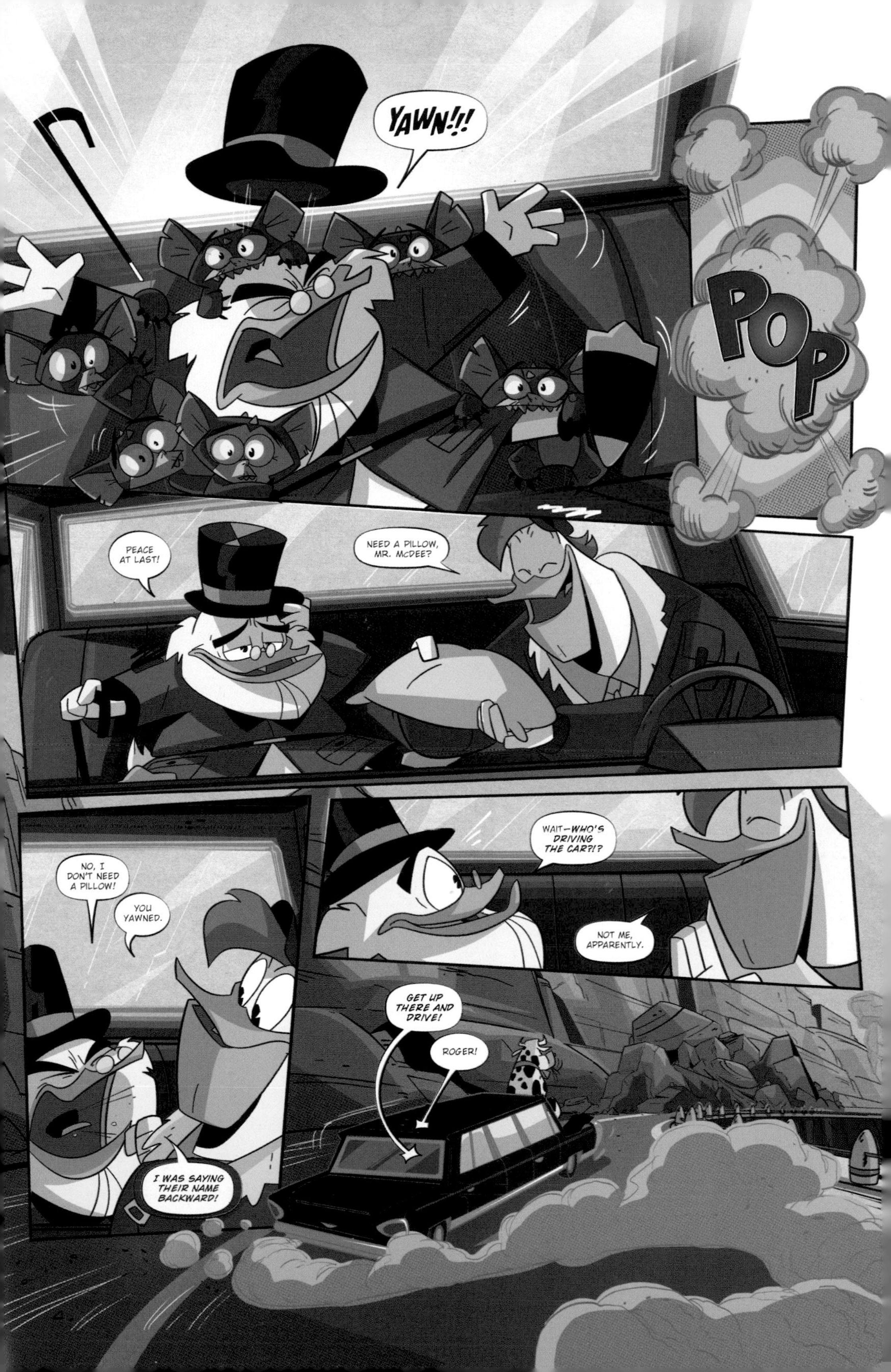

YAWN!!!
POP
PEACE AT LAST!
NEED A PILLOW, MR. McDEE?
NO, I DON'T NEED A PILLOW!
YOU YAWNED.
I WAS SAYING THEIR NAME BACKWARD!
WAIT—WHO'S DRIVING THE CAR?!?
NOT ME, APPARENTLY.
GET UP THERE AND DRIVE!
ROGER!

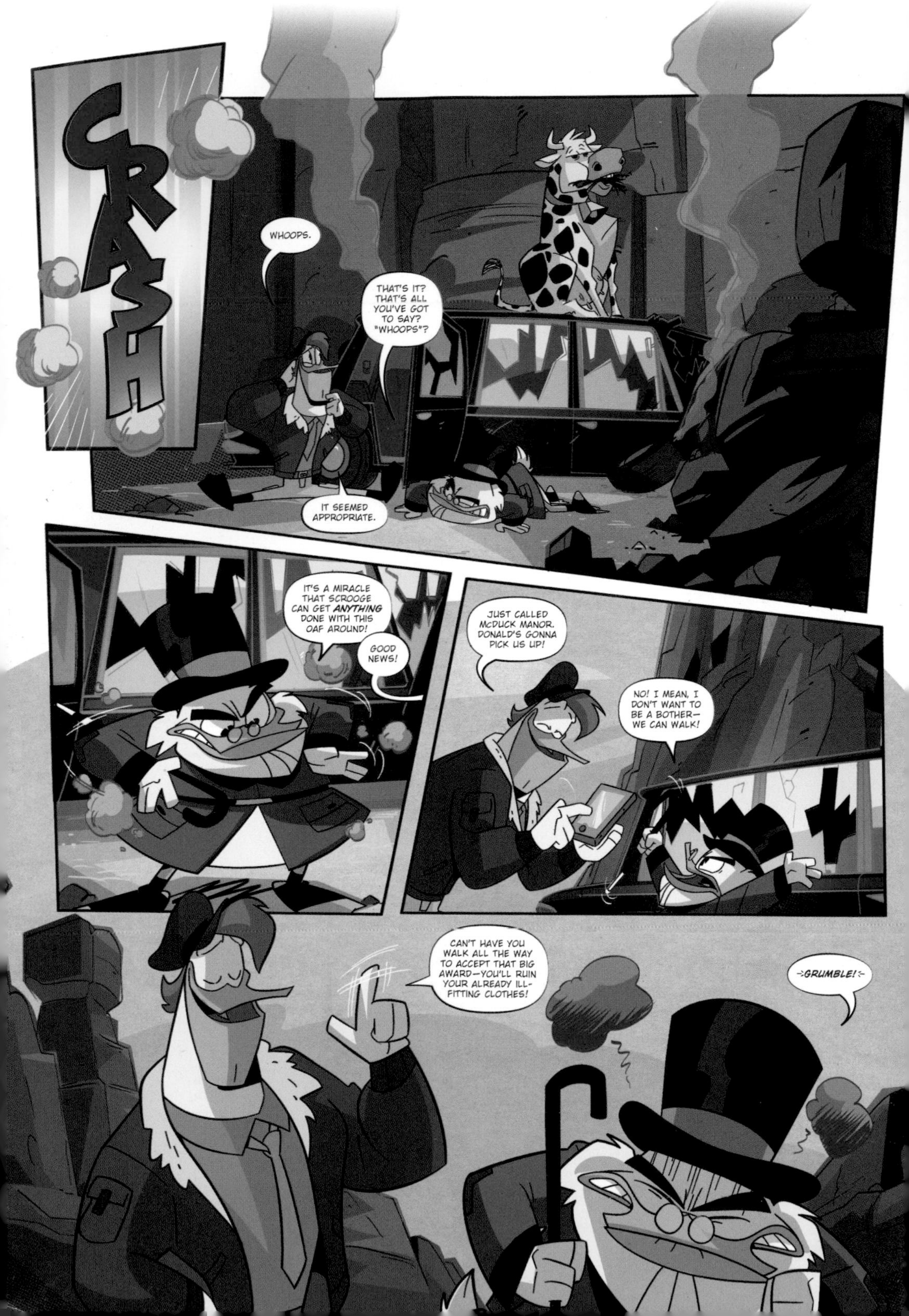
CRASH
WHOOPS.
THAT'S IT? THAT'S ALL YOU'VE GOT TO SAY? "WHOOPS"?
IT SEEMED APPROPRIATE.
IT'S A MIRACLE THAT SCROOGE CAN GET ANYTHING DONE WITH THIS OAF AROUND!
GOOD NEWS!
JUST CALLED McDUCK MANOR. DONALD'S GONNA PICK US UP!
NO! I MEAN, I DON'T WANT TO BE A BOTHER— WE CAN WALK!
CAN'T HAVE YOU WALK ALL THE WAY TO ACCEPT THAT BIG AWARD—YOU'LL RUIN YOUR ALREADY ILL-FITTING CLOTHES!
GRUMBLE!

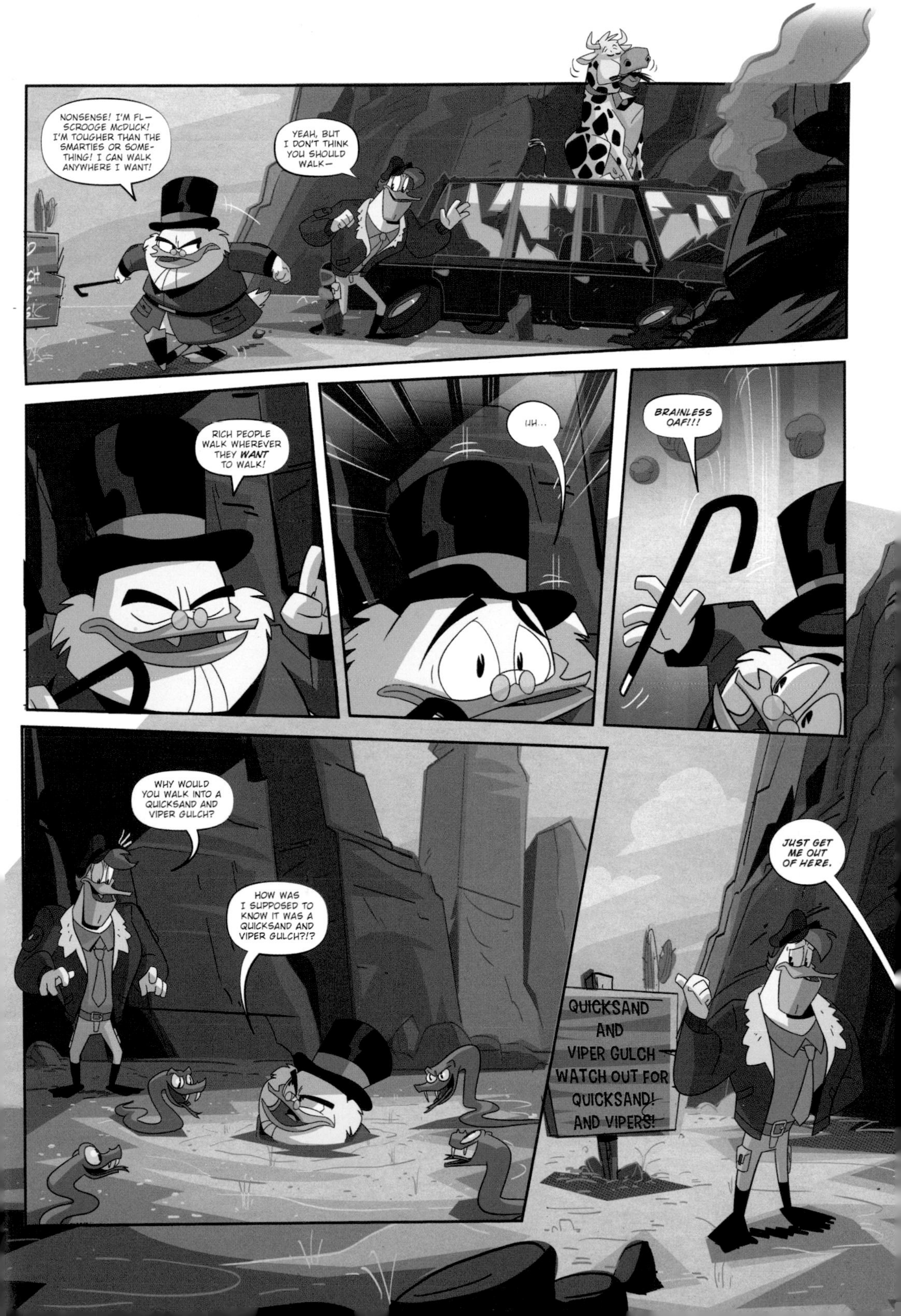
NONSENSE! I'M FL— SCROOGE McDUCK! I'M TOUGHER THAN THE SMARTIES OR SOMETHING! I CAN WALK ANYWHERE I WANT!
YEAH, BUT I DON'T THINK YOU SHOULD WALK—
RICH PEOPLE WALK WHEREVER THEY WANT TO WALK!
UH...
BRAINLESS OAF!!!
WHY WOULD YOU WALK INTO A QUICKSAND AND VIPER GULCH?
HOW WAS I SUPPOSED TO KNOW IT WAS A QUICKSAND AND VIPER GULCH?!?
QUICKSAND AND VIPER GULCH WATCH OUT FOR QUICKSAND! AND VIPERS!
JUST GET ME OUT OF HERE.

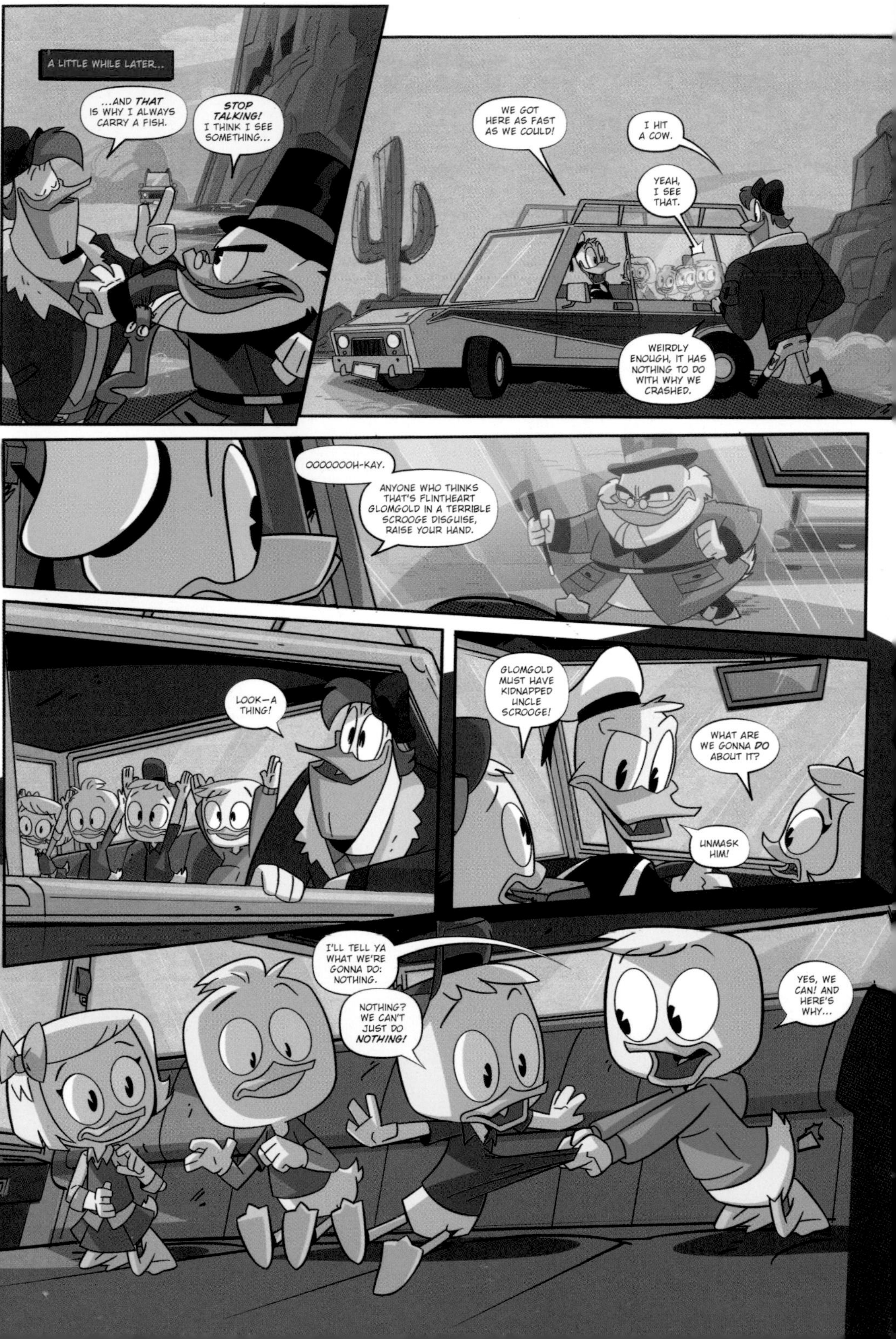
A LITTLE WHILE LATER...
...AND THAT IS WHY I ALWAYS CARRY A FISH.
STOP TALKING! I THINK I SEE SOMETHING...
WE GOT HERE AS FAST AS WE COULD!
I HIT A COW.
YEAH, I SEE THAT.
WEIRDLY ENOUGH, IT HAS NOTHING TO DO WITH WHY WE CRASHED.
OOOOOOOH-KAY.
ANYONE WHO THINKS THAT'S FLINTHEART GLOMGOLD IN A TERRIBLE SCROOGE DISGUISE, RAISE YOUR HAND.
LOOK—A THING!
GLOMGOLD MUST HAVE KIDNAPPED UNCLE SCROOGE!
WHAT ARE WE GONNA DO ABOUT IT?
UNMASK HIM!
I'LL TELL YA WHAT WE'RE GONNA DO: NOTHING.
NOTHING? WE CAN'T JUST DO NOTHING!
YES, WE CAN! AND HERE'S WHY...

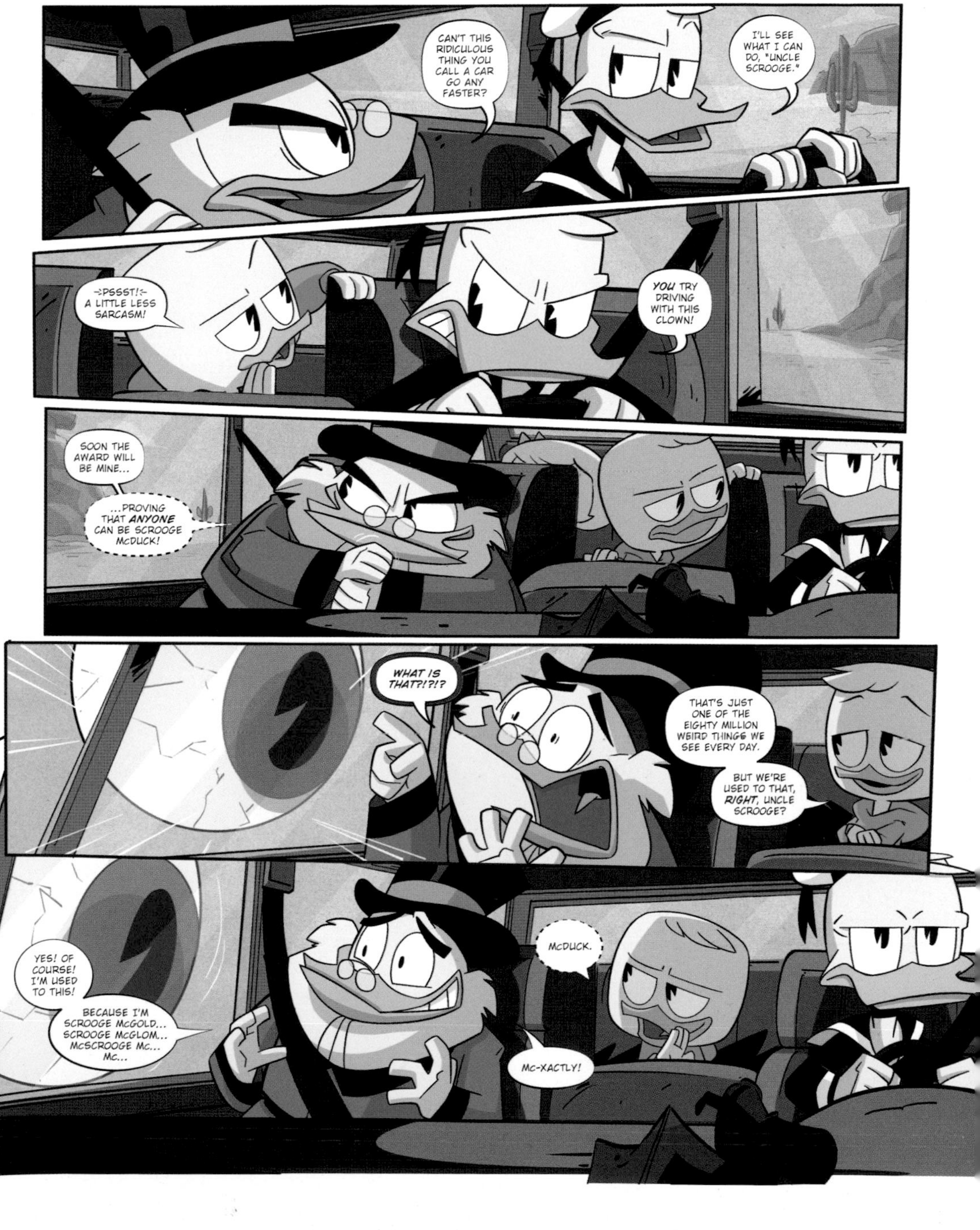
CAN'T THIS RIDICULOUS THING YOU CALL A CAR GO ANY FASTER?
I'LL SEE WHAT I CAN DO, "UNCLE SCROOGE."
-PSSST!- A LITTLE LESS SARCASM!
YOU TRY DRIVING WITH THIS CLOWN!
SOON THE AWARD WILL BE MINE...
...PROVING THAT ANYONE CAN BE SCROOGE McDUCK!
WHAT IS THAT?!?!?
THAT'S JUST ONE OF THE EIGHTY MILLION WEIRD THINGS WE SEE EVERY DAY.
BUT WE'RE USED TO THAT, RIGHT, UNCLE SCROOGE?
YES! OF COURSE! I'M USED TO THIS!
BECAUSE I'M SCROOGE McGOLD... SCROOGE McGLOM... McSCROOGE Mc... Mc...
McDUCK.
Mc-XACTLY!

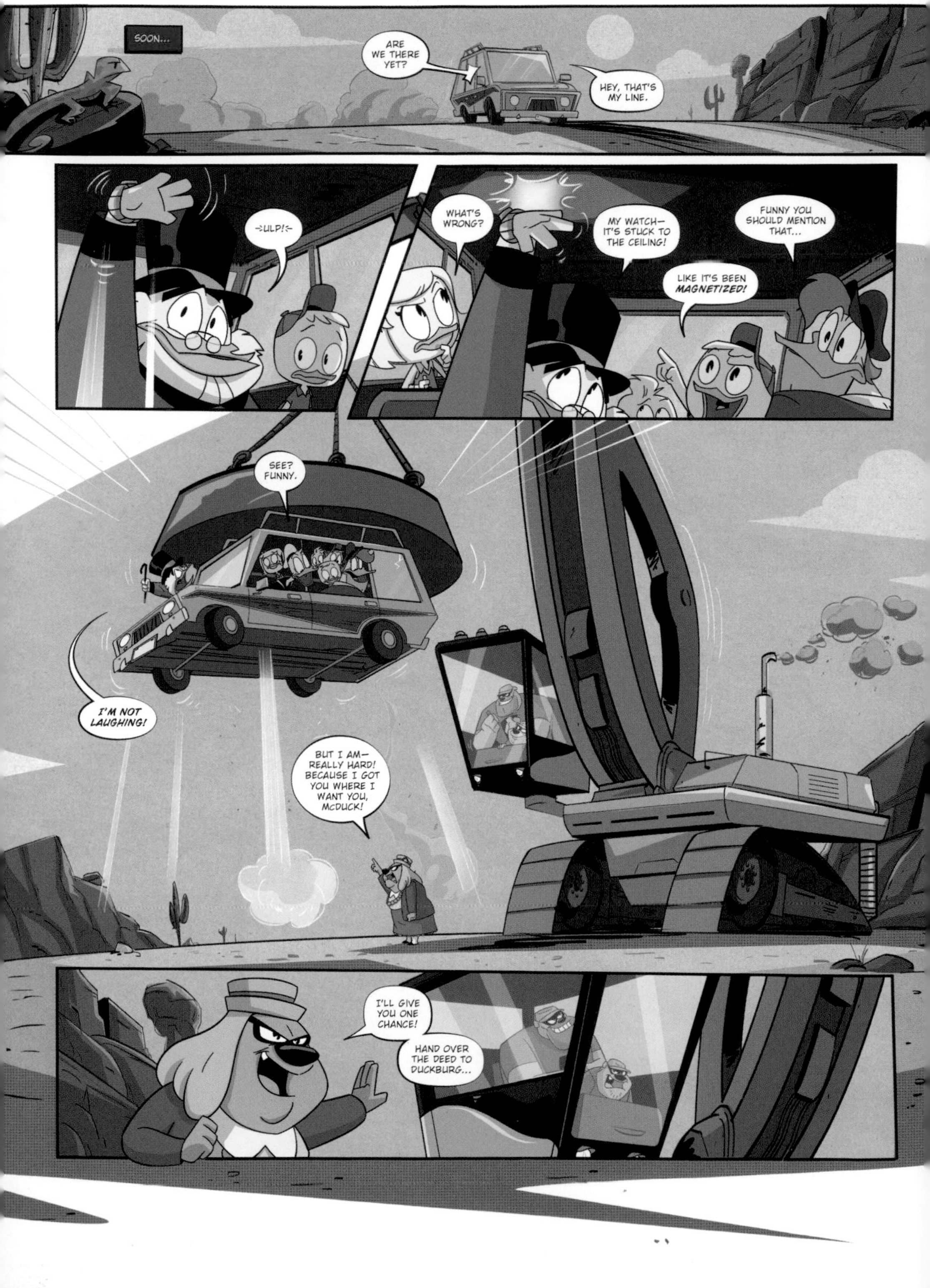
SOON...
ARE WE THERE YET?
HEY, THAT'S MY LINE.
~ULP!~
WHAT'S WRONG?
MY WATCH— IT'S STUCK TO THE CEILING!
FUNNY YOU SHOULD MENTION THAT...
LIKE IT'S BEEN MAGNETIZED!
SEE? FUNNY.
I'M NOT LAUGHING!
BUT I AM— REALLY HARD! BECAUSE I GOT YOU WHERE I WANT YOU, McDUCK!
I'LL GIVE YOU ONE CHANCE!
HAND OVER THE DEED TO DUCKBURG...

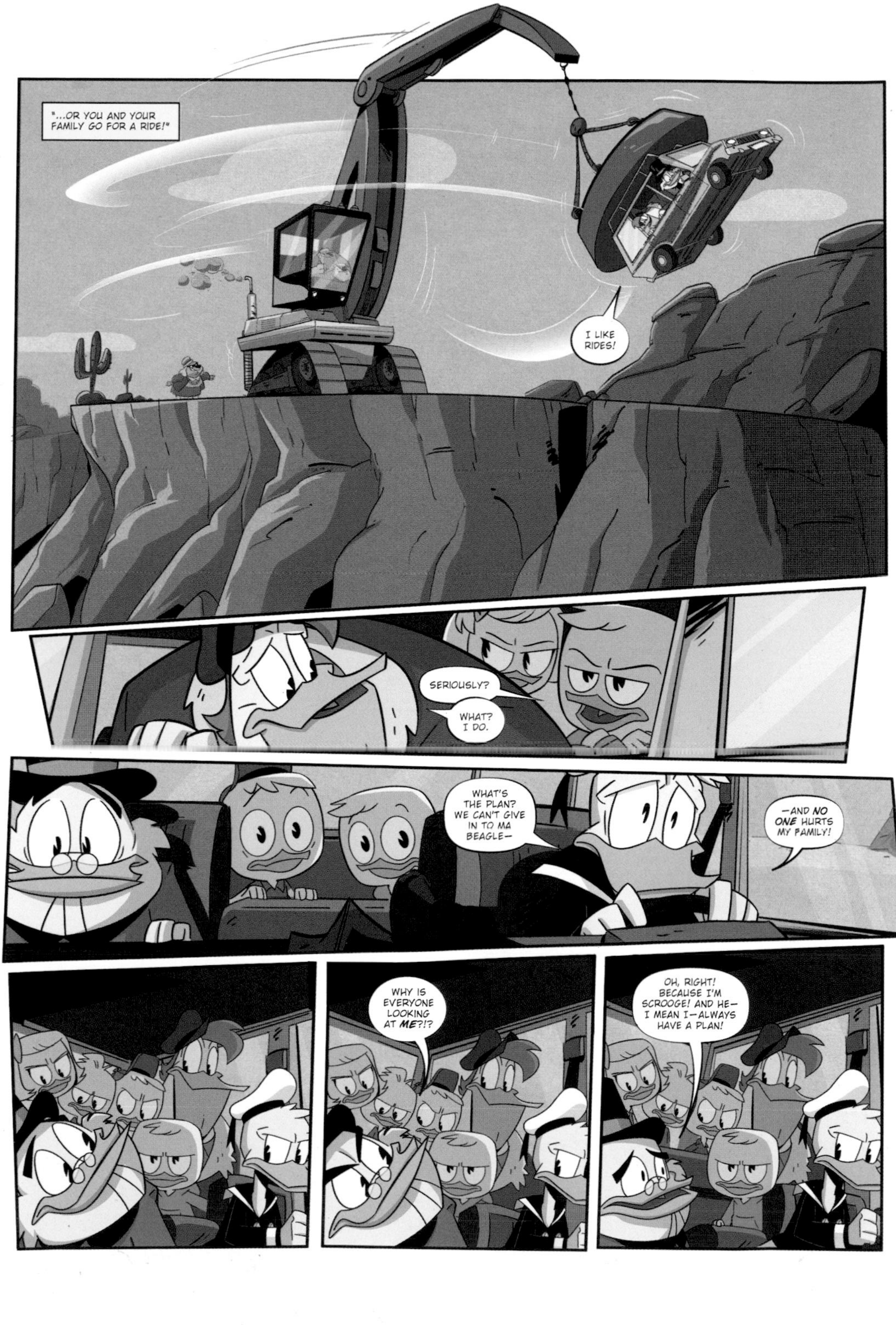
"...OR YOU AND YOUR FAMILY GO FOR A RIDE!"
I LIKE RIDES!
SERIOUSLY?
WHAT? I DO.
WHAT'S THE PLAN? WE CAN'T GIVE IN TO MA BEAGLE—
—AND NO ONE HURTS MY FAMILY!
WHY IS EVERYONE LOOKING AT ME?!?
OH, RIGHT! BECAUSE I'M SCROOGE! AND HE— I MEAN I—ALWAYS HAVE A PLAN!

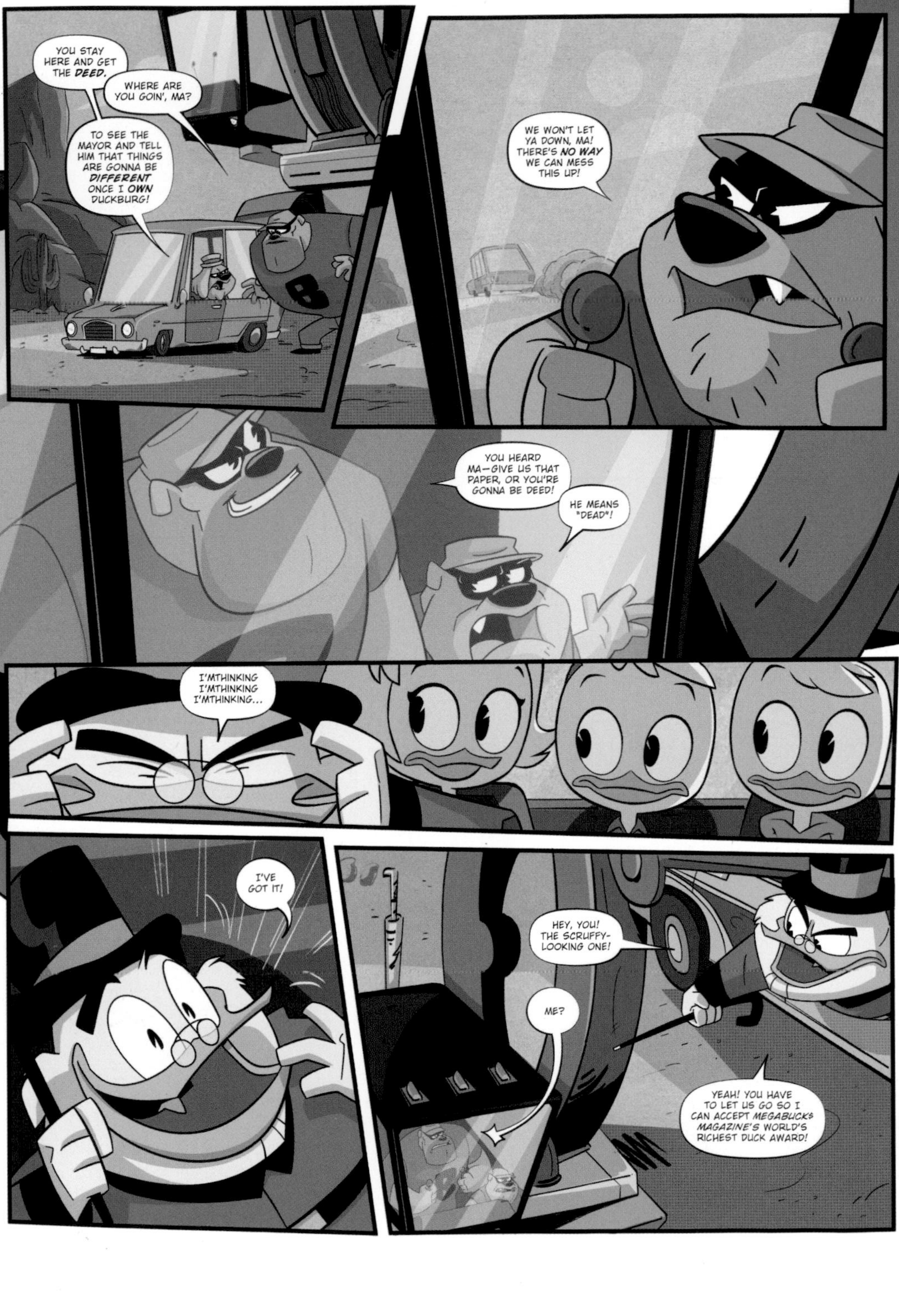

YOU STAY HERE AND GET THE DEED.
WHERE ARE YOU GOIN', MA?
TO SEE THE MAYOR AND TELL HIM THAT THINGS ARE GONNA BE DIFFERENT ONCE I OWN DUCKBURG!
WE WON'T LET YA DOWN, MA! THERE'S NO WAY WE CAN MESS THIS UP!
YOU HEARD MA—GIVE US THAT PAPER, OR YOU'RE GONNA BE DEED!
HE MEANS "DEAD"!
I'MTHINKING I'MTHINKING I'MTHINKING...
I'VE GOT IT!
HEY, YOU! THE SCRUFFY-LOOKING ONE!
ME?
YEAH! YOU HAVE TO LET US GO SO I CAN ACCEPT MEGABUCKS MAGAZINE'S WORLD'S RICHEST DUCK AWARD!

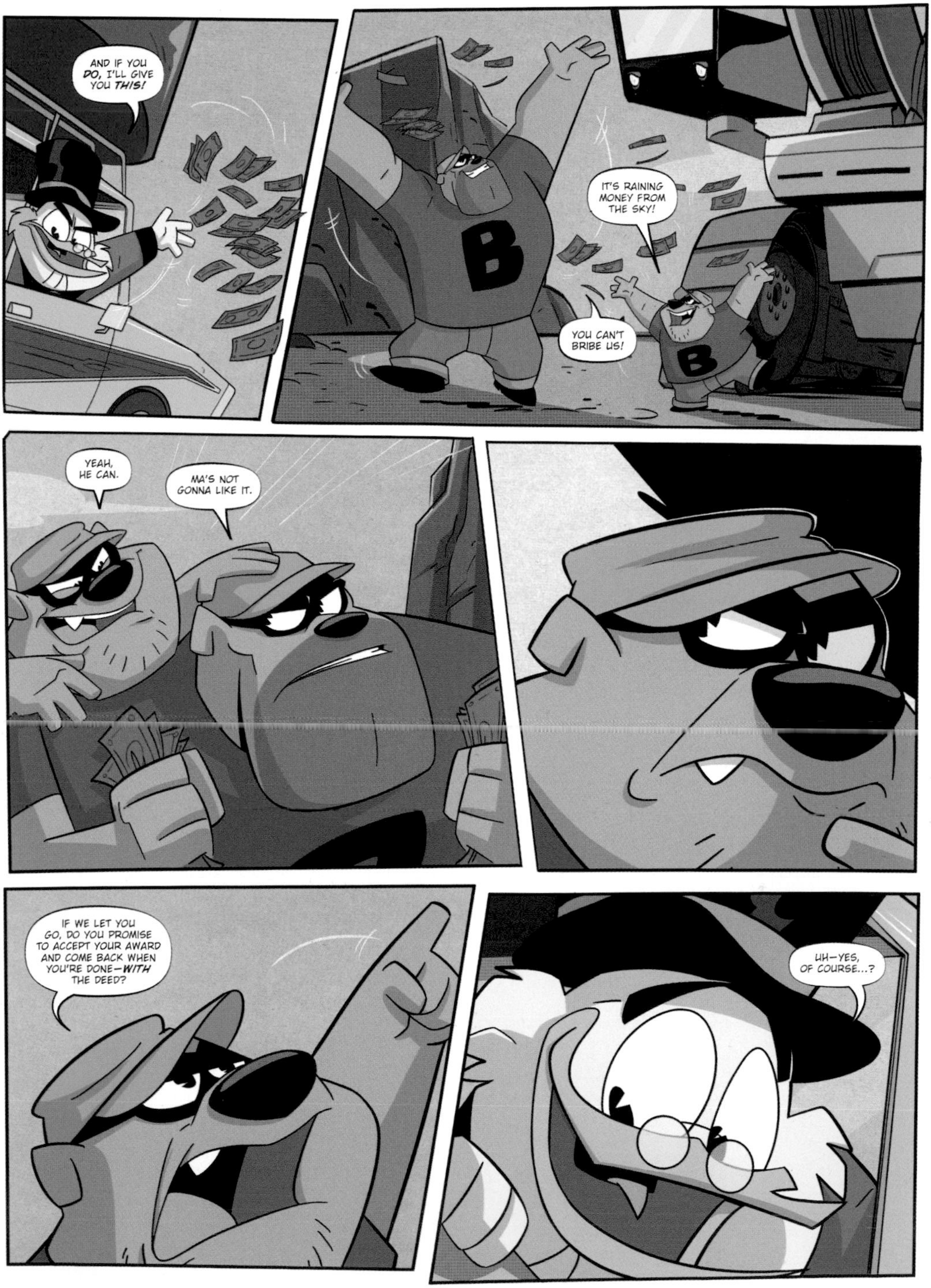
AND IF YOU DO, I'LL GIVE YOU THIS!
IT'S RAINING MONEY FROM THE SKY!
YOU CAN'T BRIBE US!
YEAH, HE CAN.
MA'S NOT GONNA LIKE IT.
IF WE LET YOU GO, DO YOU PROMISE TO ACCEPT YOUR AWARD AND COME BACK WHEN YOU'RE DONE—WITH THE DEED?
UH—YES, OF COURSE...?

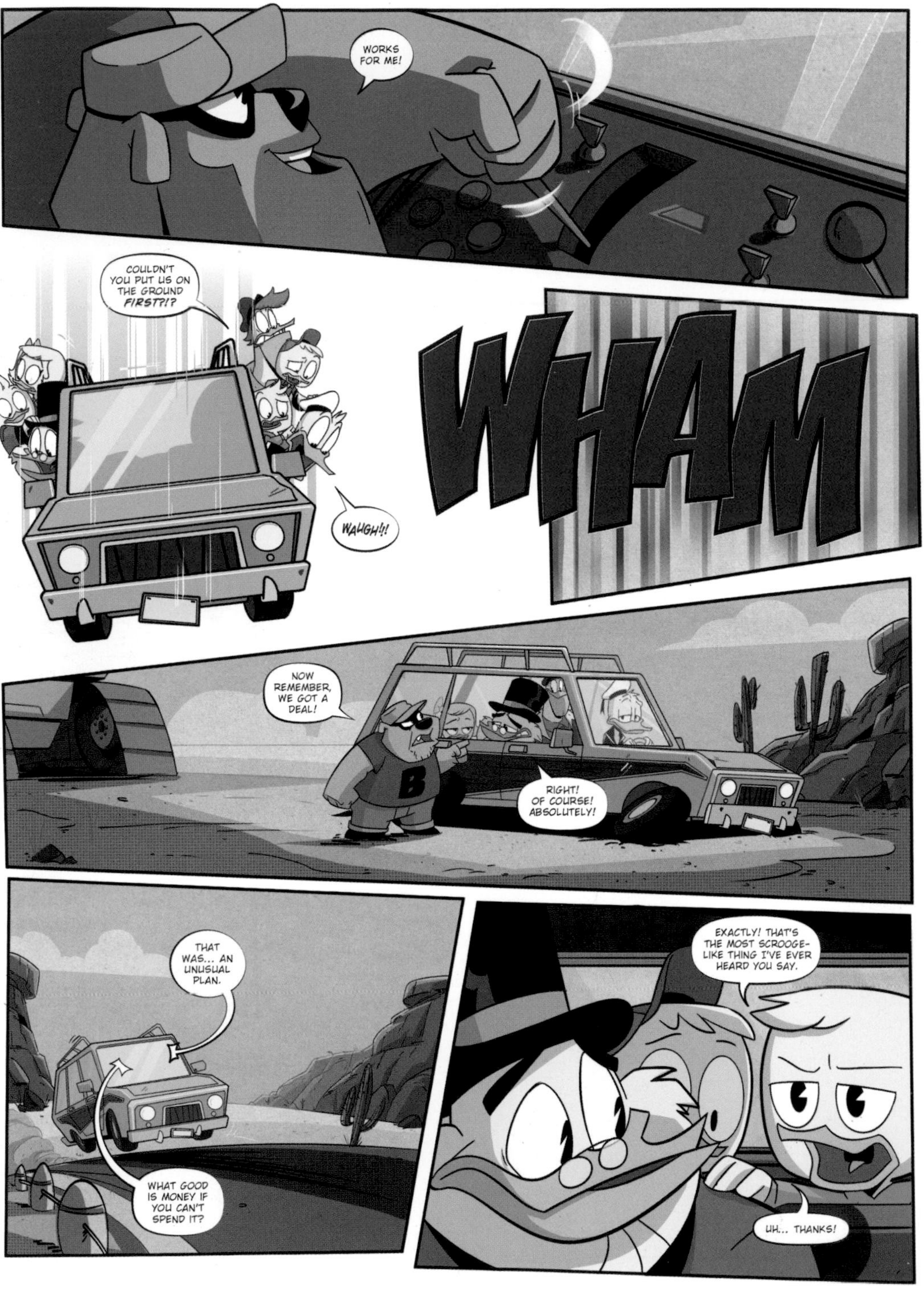
WORKS FOR ME!
COULDN'T YOU PUT US ON THE GROUND FIRST?!?
WAUGH!!!
WHAM
NOW REMEMBER, WE GOT A DEAL!
RIGHT! OF COURSE! ABSOLUTELY!
THAT WAS... AN UNUSUAL PLAN.
WHAT GOOD IS MONEY IF YOU CAN'T SPEND IT?
EXACTLY! THAT'S THE MOST SCROOGE-LIKE THING I'VE EVER HEARD YOU SAY.
UH... THANKS!

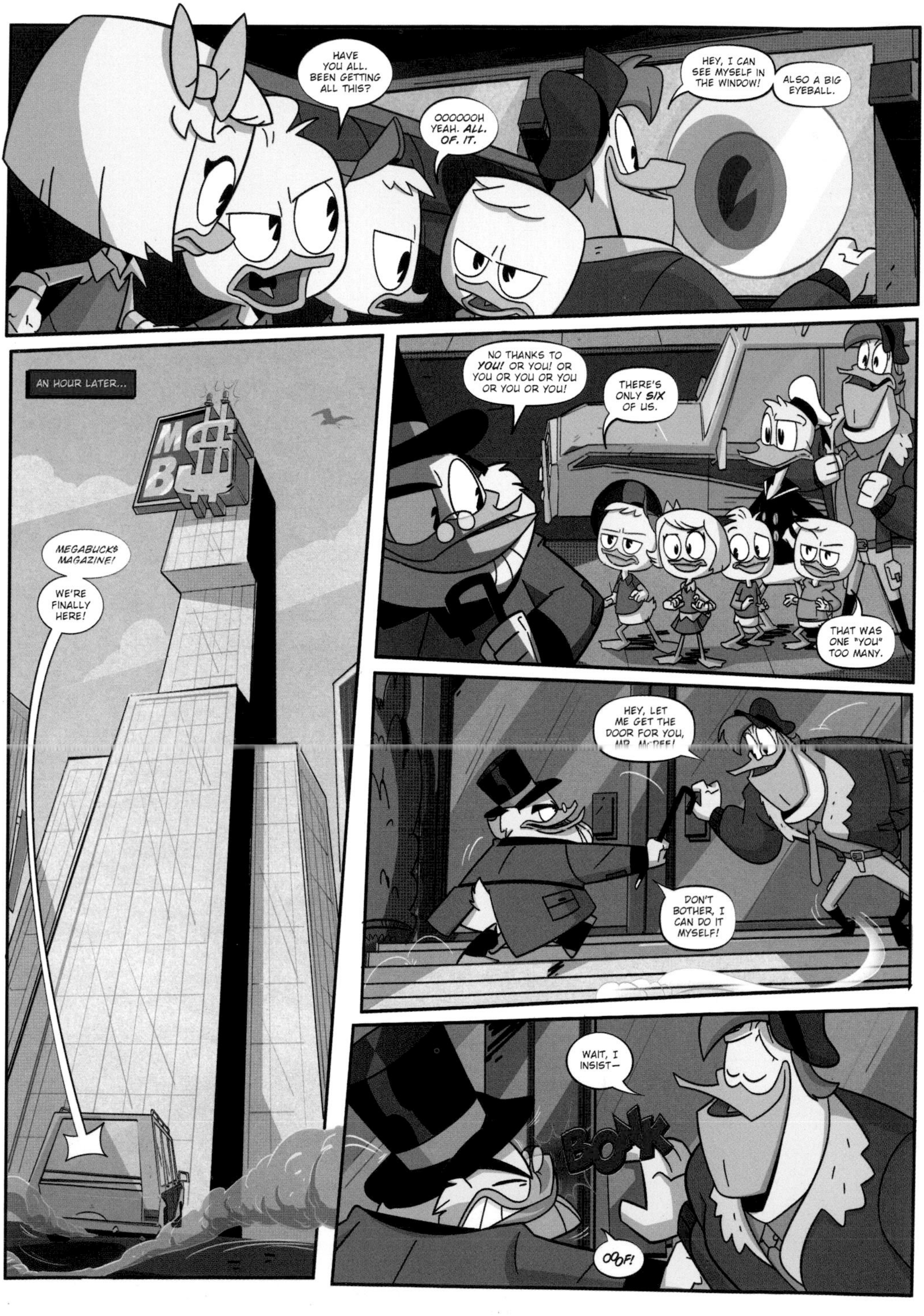
HAVE YOU ALL. BEEN GETTING ALL THIS?
OOOOOOH YEAH. ALL. OF. IT.
HEY, I CAN SEE MYSELF IN THE WINDOW!
ALSO A BIG EYEBALL.
AN HOUR LATER...
MB$
MEGABUCKS MAGAZINE!
WE'RE FINALLY HERE!
NO THANKS TO YOU! OR YOU! OR YOU OR YOU OR YOU OR YOU OR YOU!
THERE'S ONLY SIX OF US.
THAT WAS ONE "YOU" TOO MANY.
HEY, LET ME GET THE DOOR FOR YOU,
DON'T BOTHER, I CAN DO IT MYSELF!
WAIT, I INSIST—
BONK
OOOF!

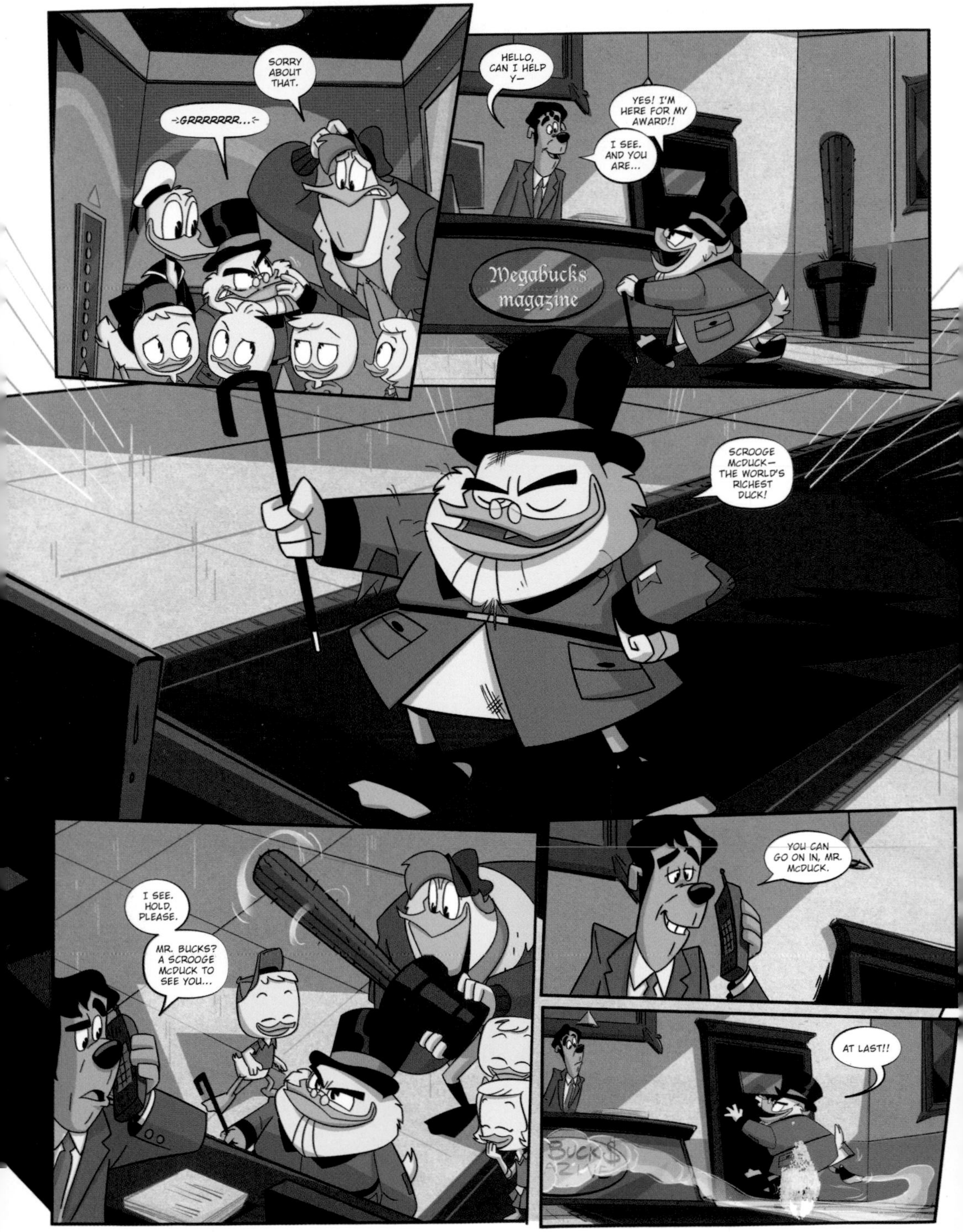
SORRY ABOUT THAT.
GRRRRRRR...
HELLO, CAN I HELP Y—
YES! I'M HERE FOR MY AWARD!!
I SEE. AND YOU ARE...
Megabucks magazine
SCROOGE McDUCK— THE WORLD'S RICHEST DUCK!
I SEE. HOLD, PLEASE.
MR. BUCKS? A SCROOGE McDUCK TO SEE YOU...
YOU CAN GO ON IN, MR. McDUCK.
AT LAST!!

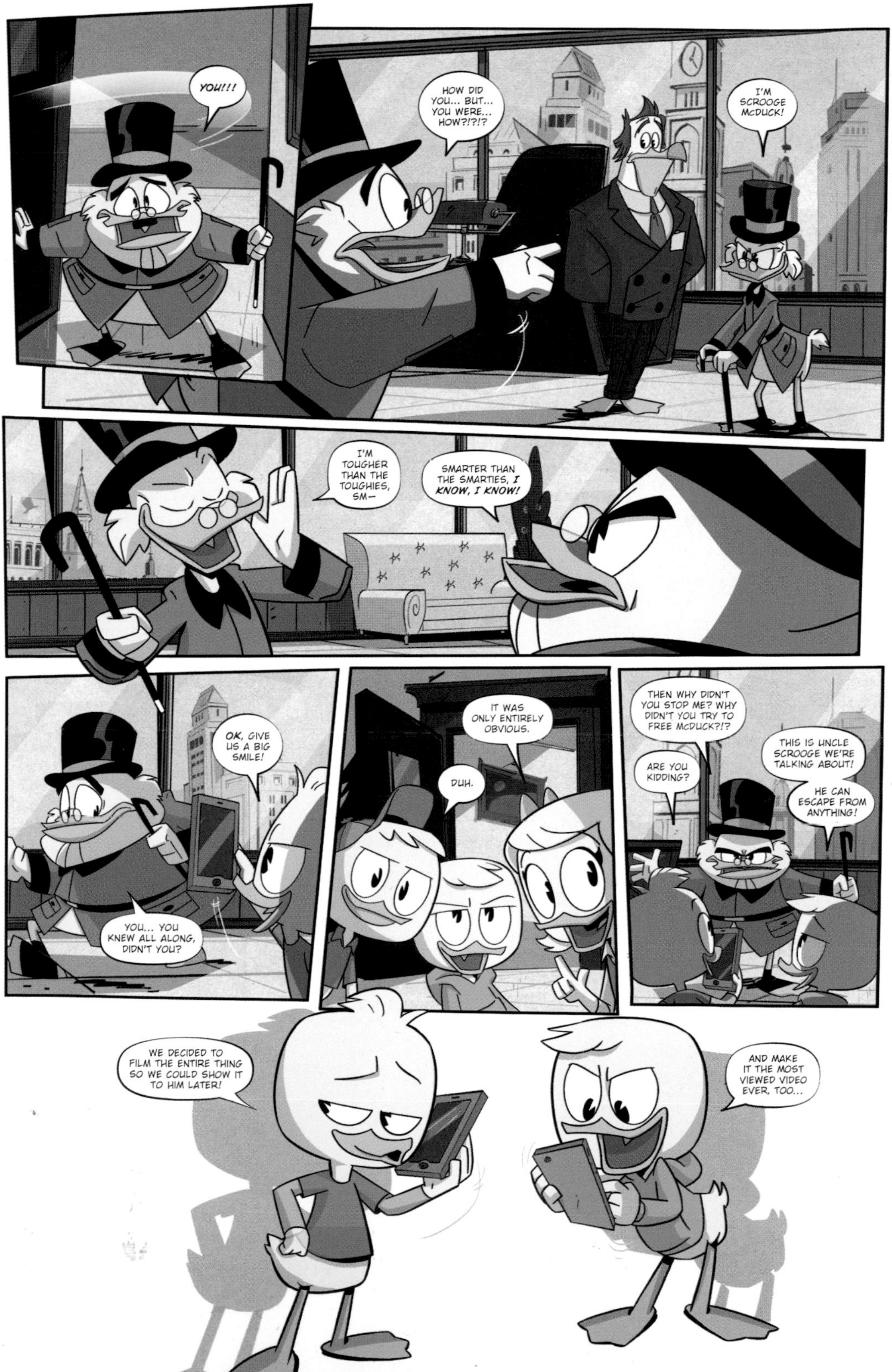
YOU!!!
HOW DID YOU... BUT... YOU WERE... HOW?!?!?
I'M SCROOGE McDUCK!
I'M TOUGHER THAN THE TOUGHIES, SM—
SMARTER THAN THE SMARTIES, *I KNOW, I KNOW!*
OK, GIVE US A BIG SMILE!
YOU... YOU KNEW ALL ALONG, DIDN'T YOU?
IT WAS ONLY ENTIRELY OBVIOUS.
DUH.
THEN WHY DIDN'T YOU STOP ME? WHY DIDN'T YOU TRY TO FREE McDUCK?!?
ARE YOU KIDDING?
THIS IS UNCLE SCROOGE WE'RE TALKING ABOUT!
HE CAN ESCAPE FROM ANYTHING!
WE DECIDED TO FILM THE ENTIRE THING SO WE COULD SHOW IT TO HIM LATER!
AND MAKE IT THE MOST VIEWED VIDEO EVER, TOO...

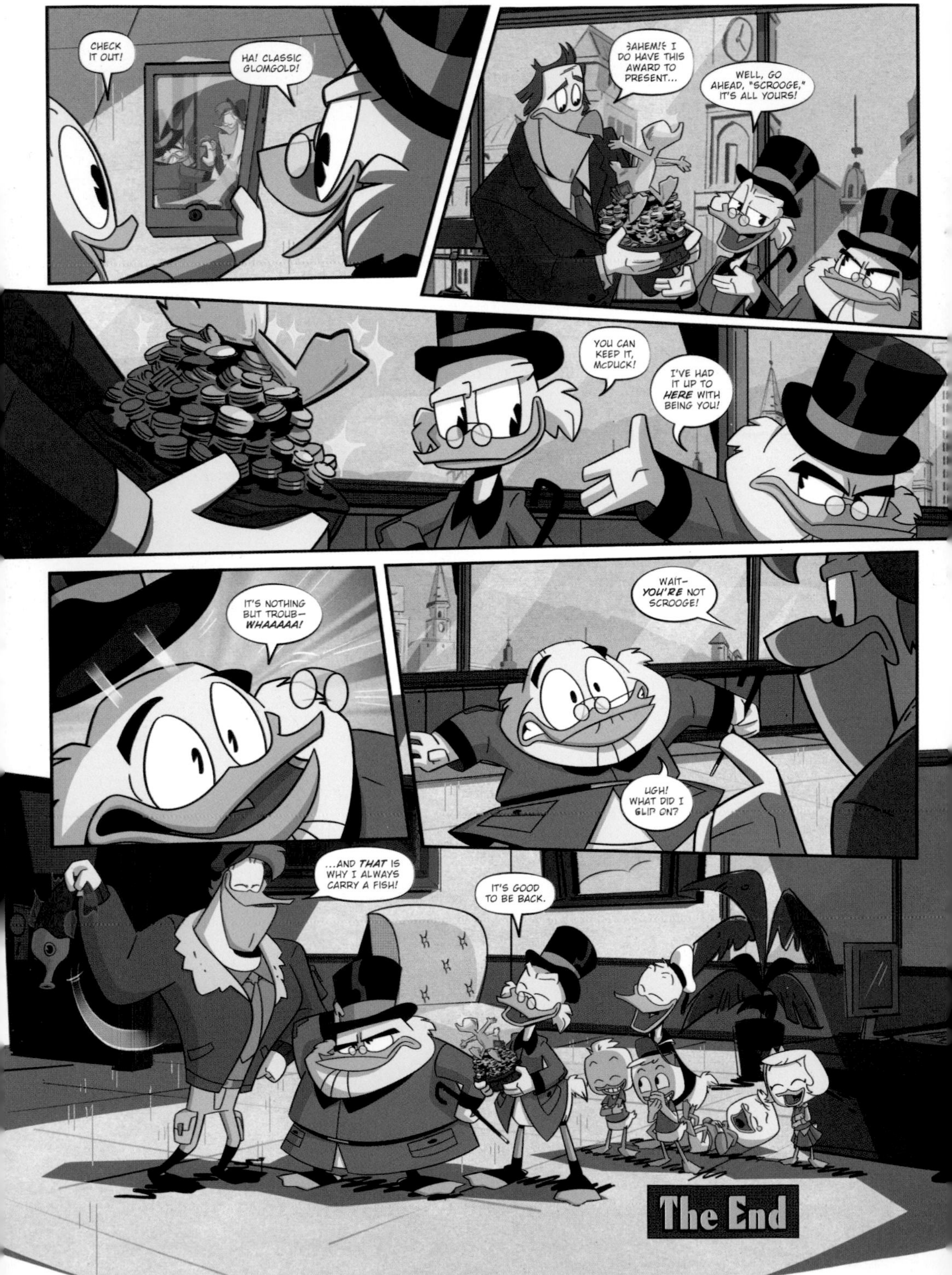
CHECK IT OUT!
HA! CLASSIC GLOMGOLD!
AHEM! I DO HAVE THIS AWARD TO PRESENT...
WELL, GO AHEAD, "SCROOGE," IT'S ALL YOURS!
YOU CAN KEEP IT, McDUCK!
I'VE HAD IT UP TO *HERE* WITH BEING YOU!
IT'S NOTHING BUT TROUB-*WHAAAAA!*
WAIT- *YOU'RE* NOT SCROOGE!
UGH! WHAT DID I SLIP ON?
...AND *THAT* IS WHY I ALWAYS CARRY A FISH!
IT'S GOOD TO BE BACK.
The End

SAGA OF THE SUPER INTERN!

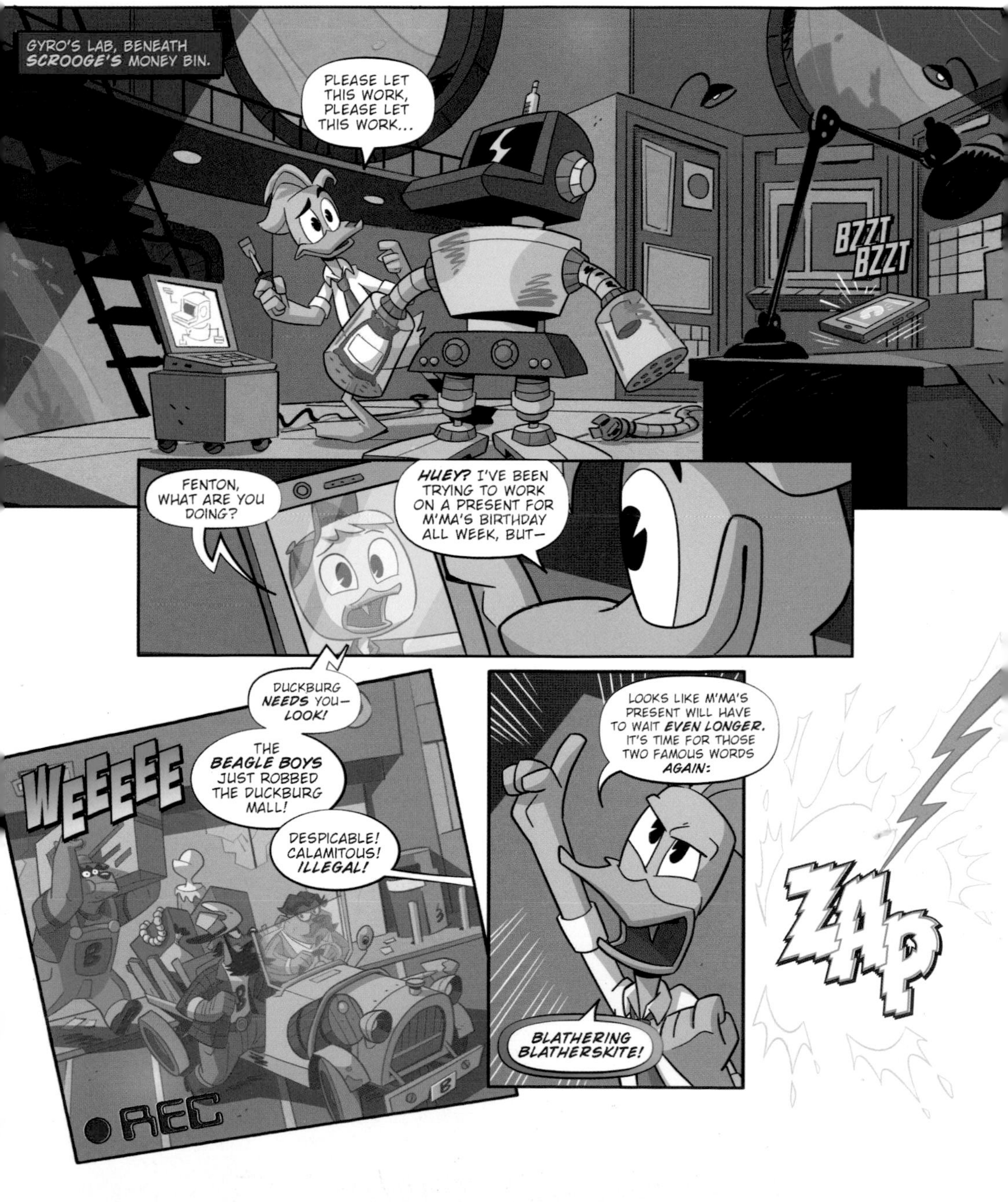
GYRO'S LAB, BENEATH SCROOGE'S MONEY BIN.
PLEASE LET THIS WORK, PLEASE LET THIS WORK...
BZZT BZZT
FENTON, WHAT ARE YOU DOING?
HUEY? I'VE BEEN TRYING TO WORK ON A PRESENT FOR M'MA'S BIRTHDAY ALL WEEK, BUT—
DUCKBURG NEEDS YOU— LOOK!
THE BEAGLE BOYS JUST ROBBED THE DUCKBURG MALL!
WEEEEE
DESPICABLE! CALAMITOUS! ILLEGAL!
REC
LOOKS LIKE M'MA'S PRESENT WILL HAVE TO WAIT EVEN LONGER. IT'S TIME FOR THOSE TWO FAMOUS WORDS AGAIN:
BLATHERING BLATHERSKITE!
ZAP

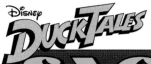

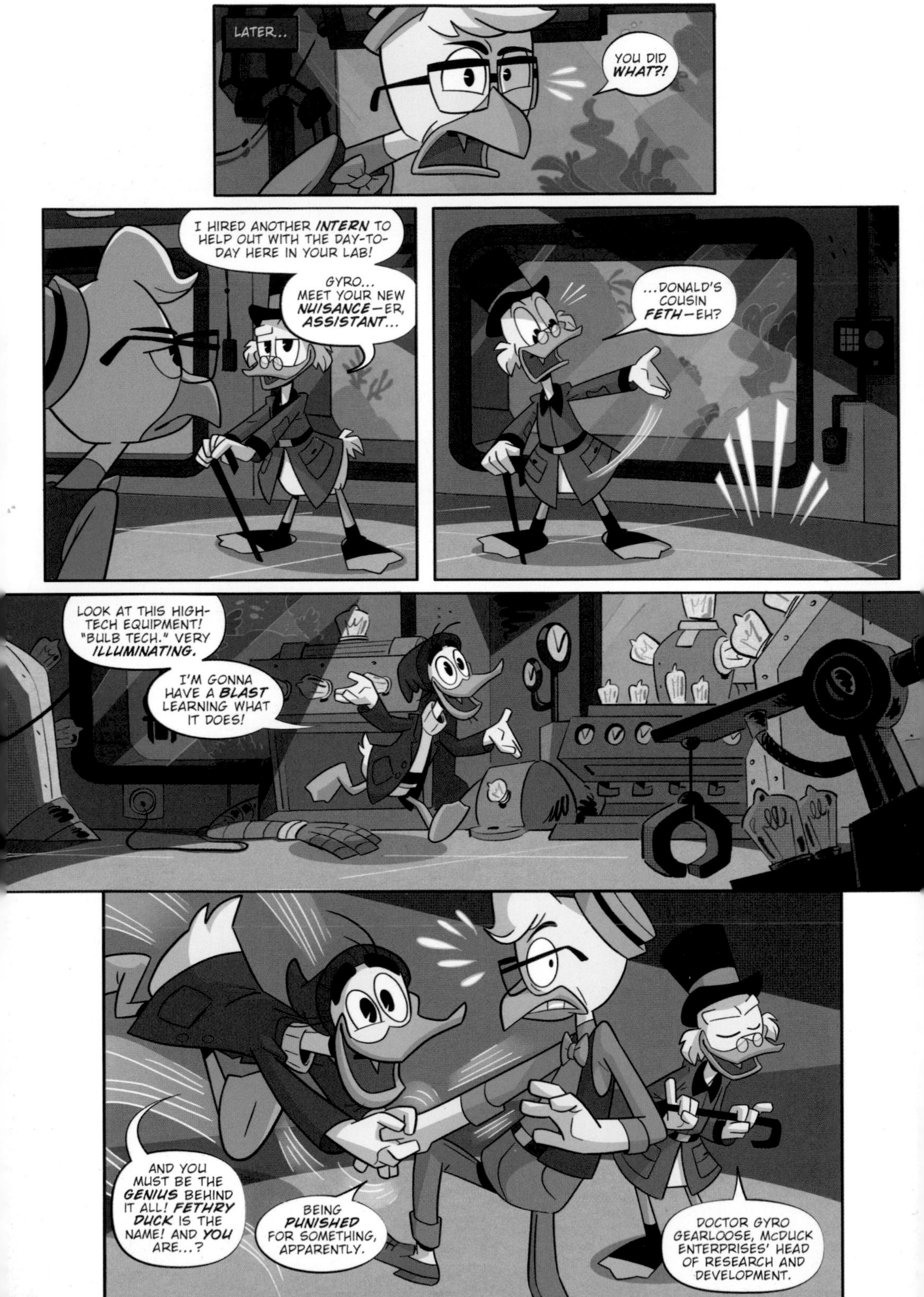
LATER...
YOU DID WHAT?!
I HIRED ANOTHER INTERN TO HELP OUT WITH THE DAY-TO-DAY HERE IN YOUR LAB!
GYRO... MEET YOUR NEW NUISANCE—ER, ASSISTANT...
...DONALD'S COUSIN FETH—EH?
LOOK AT THIS HIGH-TECH EQUIPMENT! "BULB TECH." VERY ILLUMINATING.
I'M GONNA HAVE A BLAST LEARNING WHAT IT DOES!
AND YOU MUST BE THE GENIUS BEHIND IT ALL! FETHRY DUCK IS THE NAME! AND YOU ARE...?
BEING PUNISHED FOR SOMETHING, APPARENTLY.
DOCTOR GYRO GEARLOOSE, McDUCK ENTERPRISES' HEAD OF RESEARCH AND DEVELOPMENT.

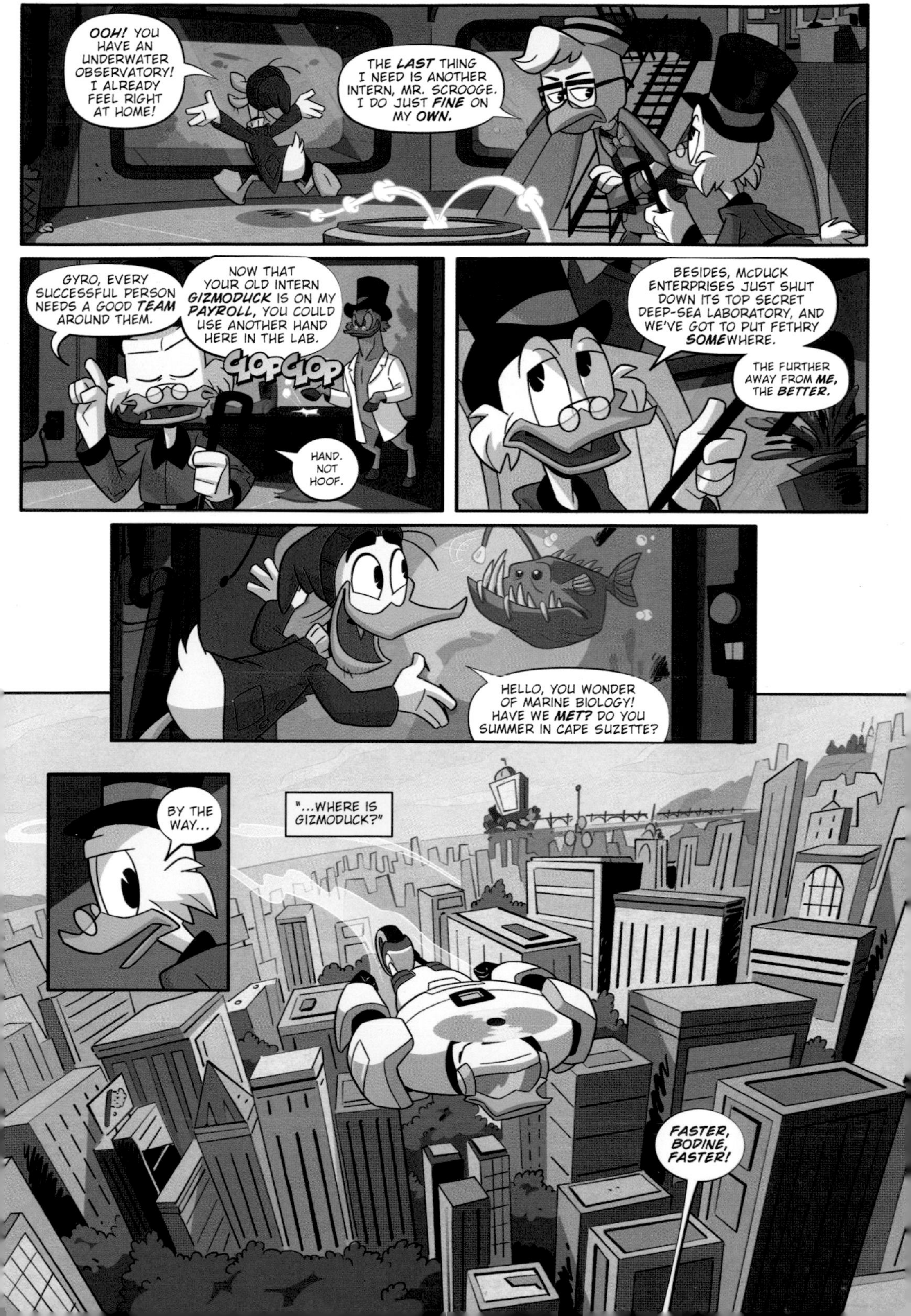
OOH! YOU HAVE AN UNDERWATER OBSERVATORY! I ALREADY FEEL RIGHT AT HOME!
THE LAST THING I NEED IS ANOTHER INTERN, MR. SCROOGE. I DO JUST FINE ON MY OWN.
GYRO, EVERY SUCCESSFUL PERSON NEEDS A GOOD TEAM AROUND THEM.
NOW THAT YOUR OLD INTERN GIZMODUCK IS ON MY PAYROLL, YOU COULD USE ANOTHER HAND HERE IN THE LAB.
CLOPCLOP
HAND. NOT HOOF.
BESIDES, McDUCK ENTERPRISES JUST SHUT DOWN ITS TOP SECRET DEEP-SEA LABORATORY, AND WE'VE GOT TO PUT FETHRY SOMEWHERE.
THE FURTHER AWAY FROM ME, THE BETTER.
HELLO, YOU WONDER OF MARINE BIOLOGY! HAVE WE MET? DO YOU SUMMER IN CAPE SUZETTE?
BY THE WAY...
"...WHERE IS GIZMODUCK?"
FASTER, BODINE, FASTER!

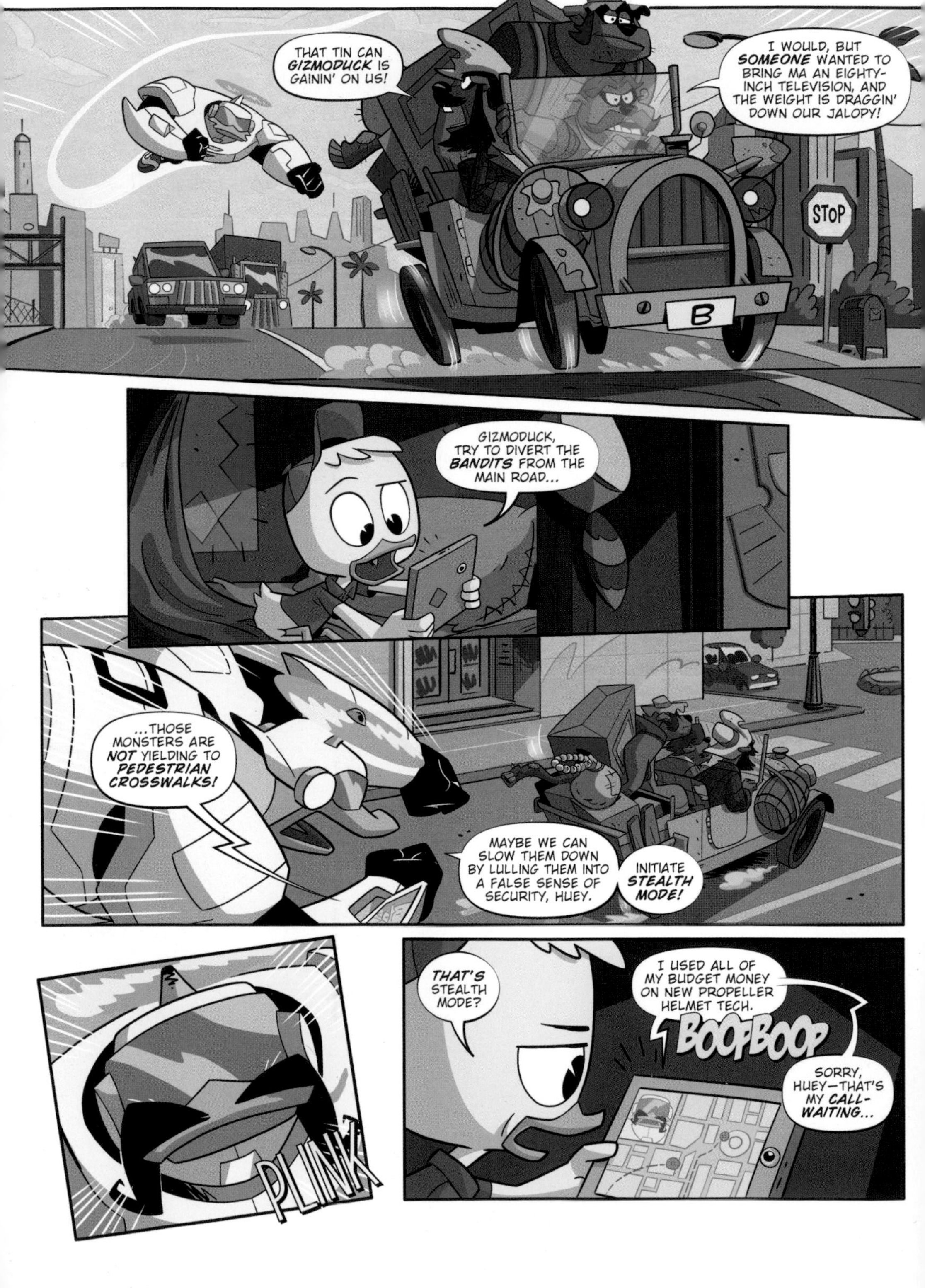

THAT TIN CAN GIZMODUCK IS GAININ' ON US!
I WOULD, BUT SOMEONE WANTED TO BRING MA AN EIGHTY-INCH TELEVISION, AND THE WEIGHT IS DRAGGIN' DOWN OUR JALOPY!
STOP
B
GIZMODUCK, TRY TO DIVERT THE BANDITS FROM THE MAIN ROAD...
...THOSE MONSTERS ARE NOT YIELDING TO PEDESTRIAN CROSSWALKS!
MAYBE WE CAN SLOW THEM DOWN BY LULLING THEM INTO A FALSE SENSE OF SECURITY, HUEY.
INITIATE STEALTH MODE!
PLINK
THAT'S STEALTH MODE?
I USED ALL OF MY BUDGET MONEY ON NEW PROPELLER HELMET TECH.
BOOPBOOP
SORRY, HUEY—THAT'S MY CALL-WAITING...

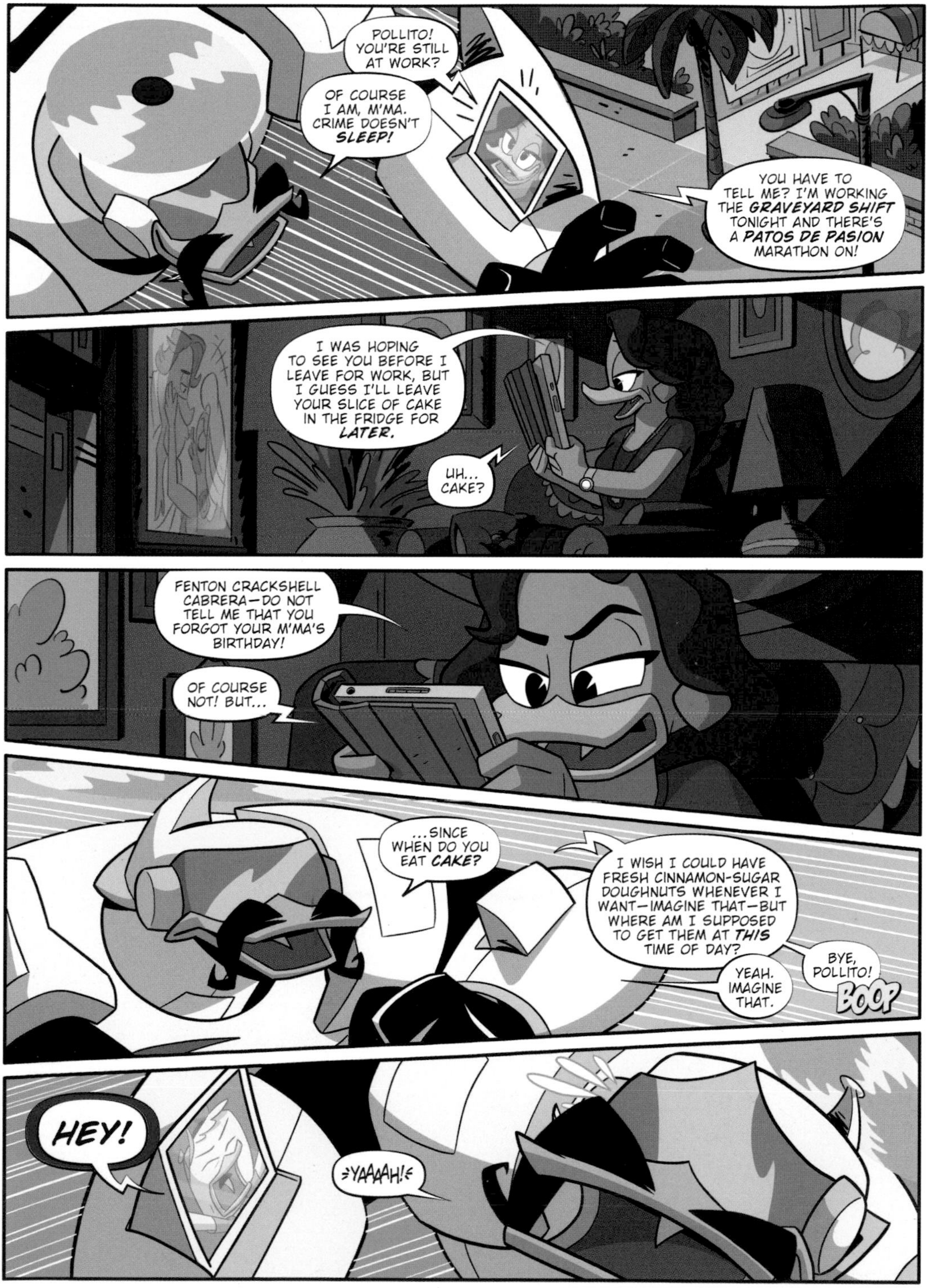
POLLITO! YOU'RE STILL AT WORK?
OF COURSE I AM, M'MA. CRIME DOESN'T SLEEP!
YOU HAVE TO TELL ME? I'M WORKING THE GRAVEYARD SHIFT TONIGHT AND THERE'S A PATOS DE PASION MARATHON ON!
I WAS HOPING TO SEE YOU BEFORE I LEAVE FOR WORK, BUT I GUESS I'LL LEAVE YOUR SLICE OF CAKE IN THE FRIDGE FOR LATER.
UH... CAKE?
FENTON CRACKSHELL CABRERA—DO NOT TELL ME THAT YOU FORGOT YOUR M'MA'S BIRTHDAY!
OF COURSE NOT! BUT...
...SINCE WHEN DO YOU EAT CAKE?
I WISH I COULD HAVE FRESH CINNAMON-SUGAR DOUGHNUTS WHENEVER I WANT—IMAGINE THAT—BUT WHERE AM I SUPPOSED TO GET THEM AT THIS TIME OF DAY?
YEAH. IMAGINE THAT.
BYE, POLLITO!
BOOP
HEY!
YAAAAH!

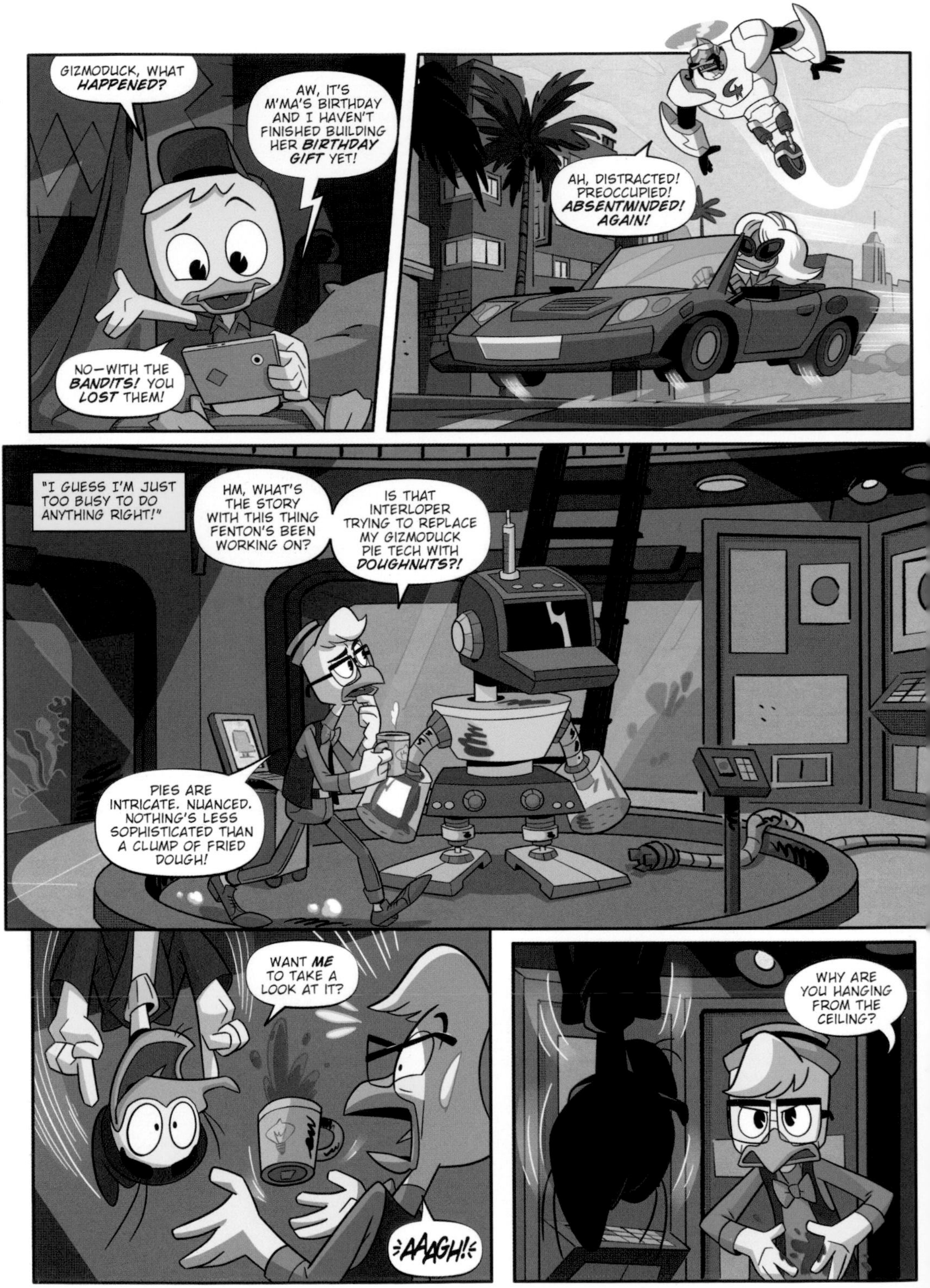
GIZMODUCK, WHAT HAPPENED?
AW, IT'S M'MA'S BIRTHDAY AND I HAVEN'T FINISHED BUILDING HER BIRTHDAY GIFT YET!
NO—WITH THE BANDITS! YOU LOST THEM!
AH, DISTRACTED! PREOCCUPIED! ABSENTMINDED! AGAIN!
"I GUESS I'M JUST TOO BUSY TO DO ANYTHING RIGHT!"
HM, WHAT'S THE STORY WITH THIS THING FENTON'S BEEN WORKING ON?
IS THAT INTERLOPER TRYING TO REPLACE MY GIZMODUCK PIE TECH WITH DOUGHNUTS?!
PIES ARE INTRICATE. NUANCED. NOTHING'S LESS SOPHISTICATED THAN A CLUMP OF FRIED DOUGH!
WANT ME TO TAKE A LOOK AT IT?
AAAGH!
WHY ARE YOU HANGING FROM THE CEILING?

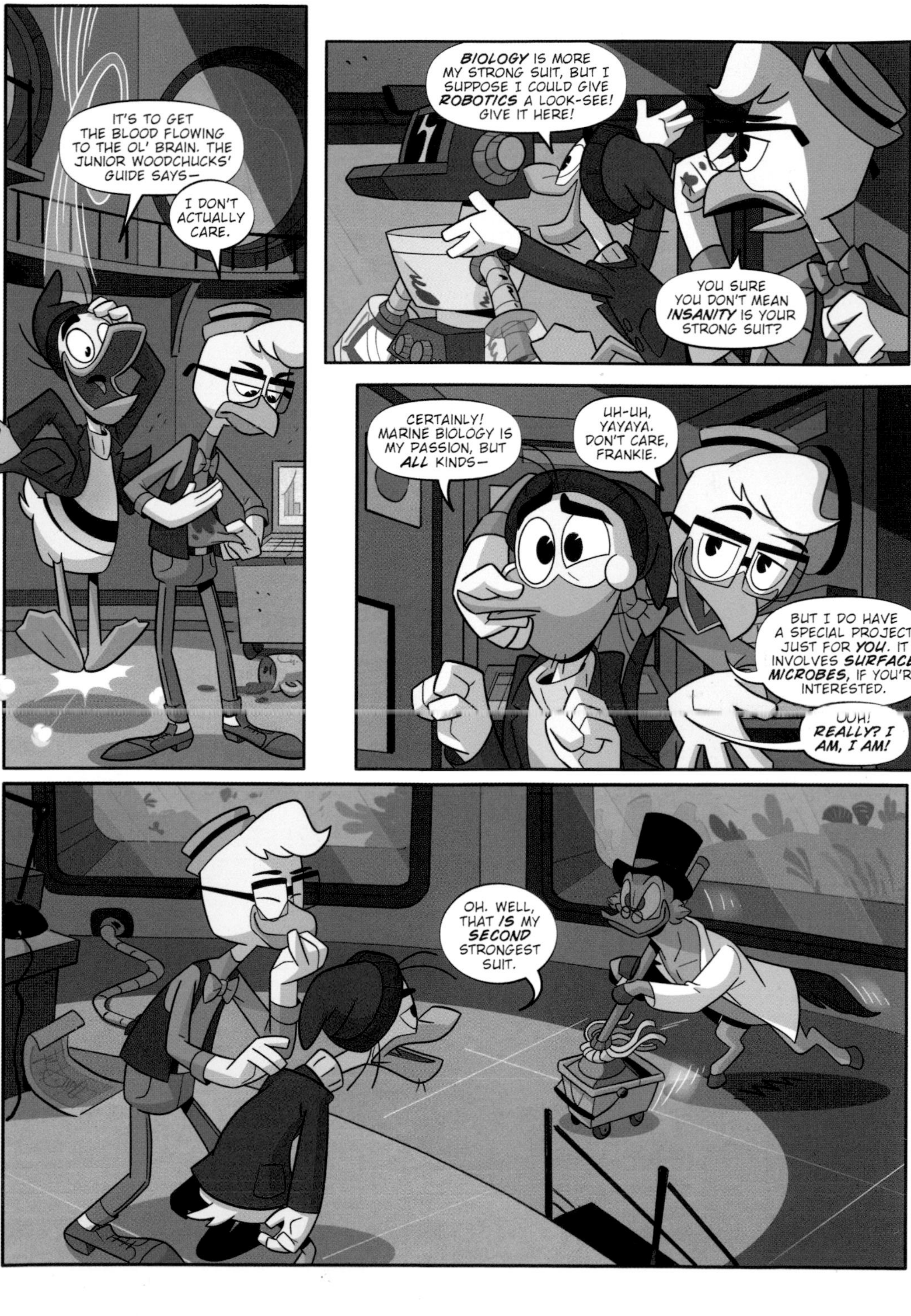
IT'S TO GET THE BLOOD FLOWING TO THE OL' BRAIN. THE JUNIOR WOODCHUCKS' GUIDE SAYS—
I DON'T ACTUALLY CARE.
BIOLOGY IS MORE MY STRONG SUIT, BUT I SUPPOSE I COULD GIVE ROBOTICS A LOOK-SEE! GIVE IT HERE!
YOU SURE YOU DON'T MEAN INSANITY IS YOUR STRONG SUIT?
CERTAINLY! MARINE BIOLOGY IS MY PASSION, BUT ALL KINDS—
UH-UH, YAYAYA. DON'T CARE, FRANKIE.
BUT I DO HAVE A SPECIAL PROJECT JUST FOR YOU. IT INVOLVES SURFACE MICROBES, IF YOU'RE INTERESTED.
OOH! REALLY? I AM, I AM!
OH. WELL, THAT IS MY SECOND STRONGEST SUIT.

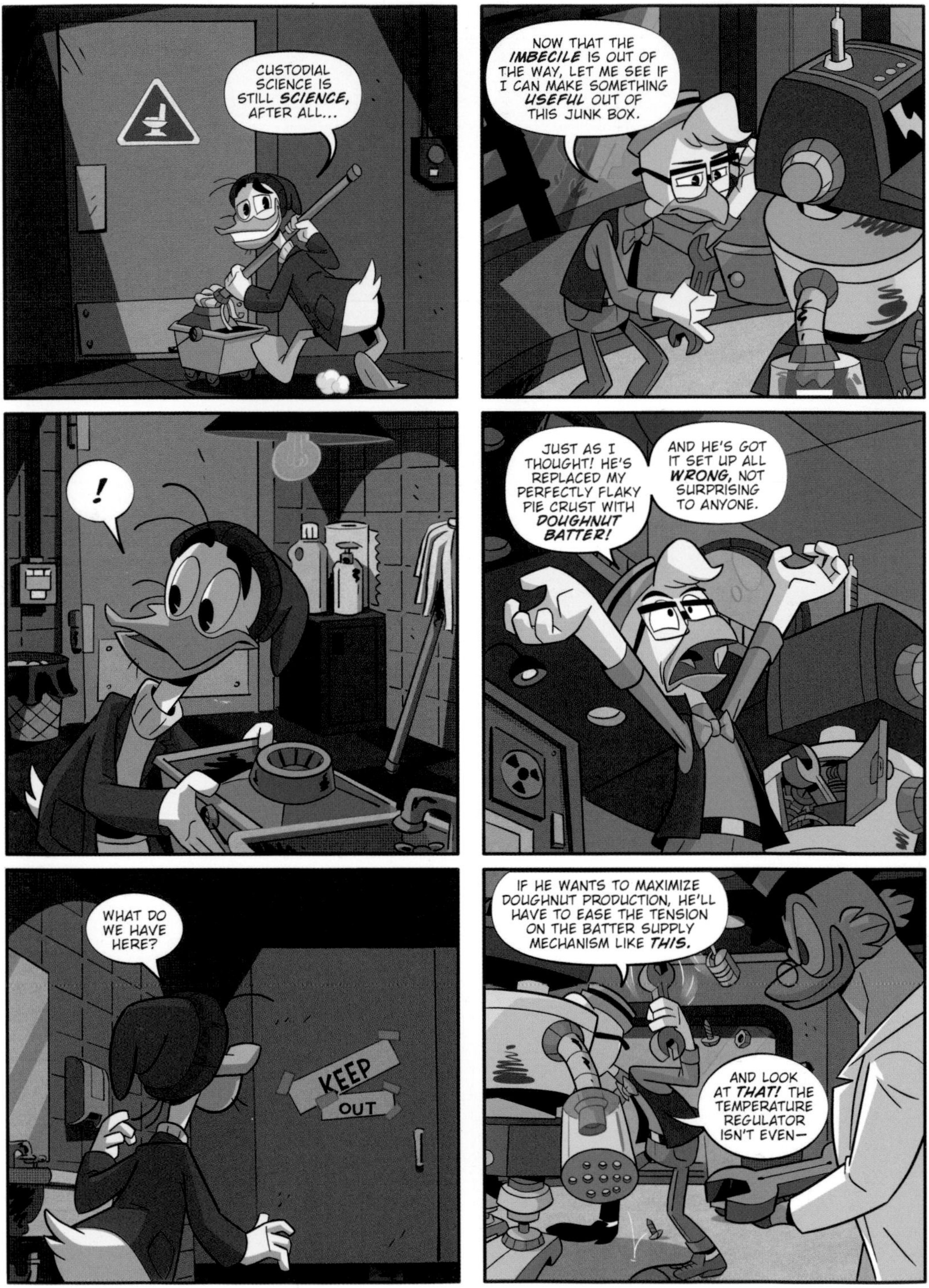
CUSTODIAL SCIENCE IS STILL SCIENCE, AFTER ALL...
NOW THAT THE IMBECILE IS OUT OF THE WAY, LET ME SEE IF I CAN MAKE SOMETHING USEFUL OUT OF THIS JUNK BOX.
!
JUST AS I THOUGHT! HE'S REPLACED MY PERFECTLY FLAKY PIE CRUST WITH DOUGHNUT BATTER!
AND HE'S GOT IT SET UP ALL WRONG, NOT SURPRISING TO ANYONE.
WHAT DO WE HAVE HERE?
KEEP
OUT
IF HE WANTS TO MAXIMIZE DOUGHNUT PRODUCTION, HE'LL HAVE TO EASE THE TENSION ON THE BATTER SUPPLY MECHANISM LIKE THIS.
AND LOOK AT THAT! THE TEMPERATURE REGULATOR ISN'T EVEN—

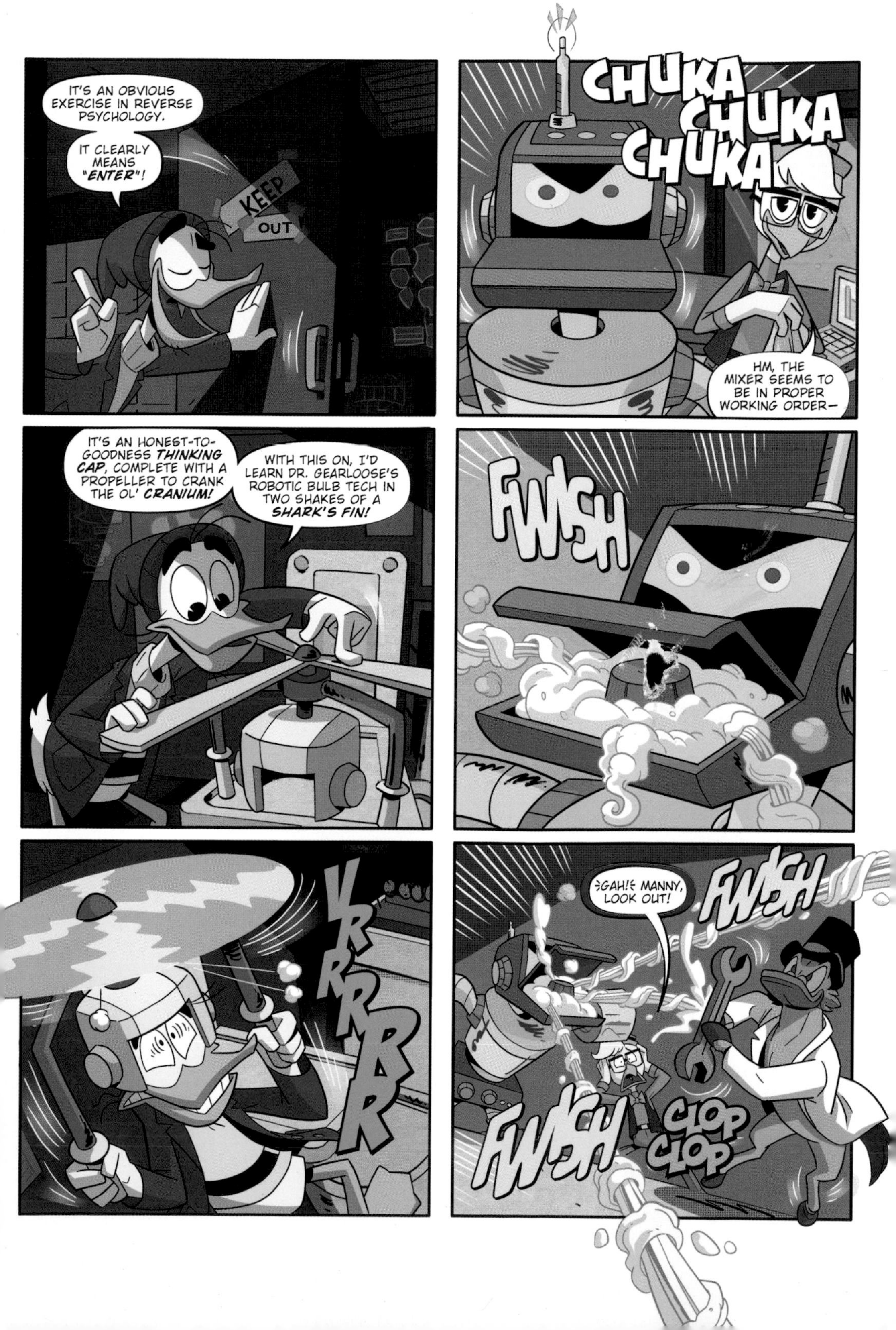
IT'S AN OBVIOUS EXERCISE IN REVERSE PSYCHOLOGY.
IT CLEARLY MEANS "ENTER"!
KEEP OUT
CHUKA CHUKA CHUKA
HM, THE MIXER SEEMS TO BE IN PROPER WORKING ORDER—
IT'S AN HONEST-TO-GOODNESS THINKING CAP, COMPLETE WITH A PROPELLER TO CRANK THE OL' CRANIUM!
WITH THIS ON, I'D LEARN DR. GEARLOOSE'S ROBOTIC BULB TECH IN TWO SHAKES OF A SHARK'S FIN!
FWISH
VRRRRR
GAH! MANNY, LOOK OUT!
FWISH
FWISH
CLOP CLOP

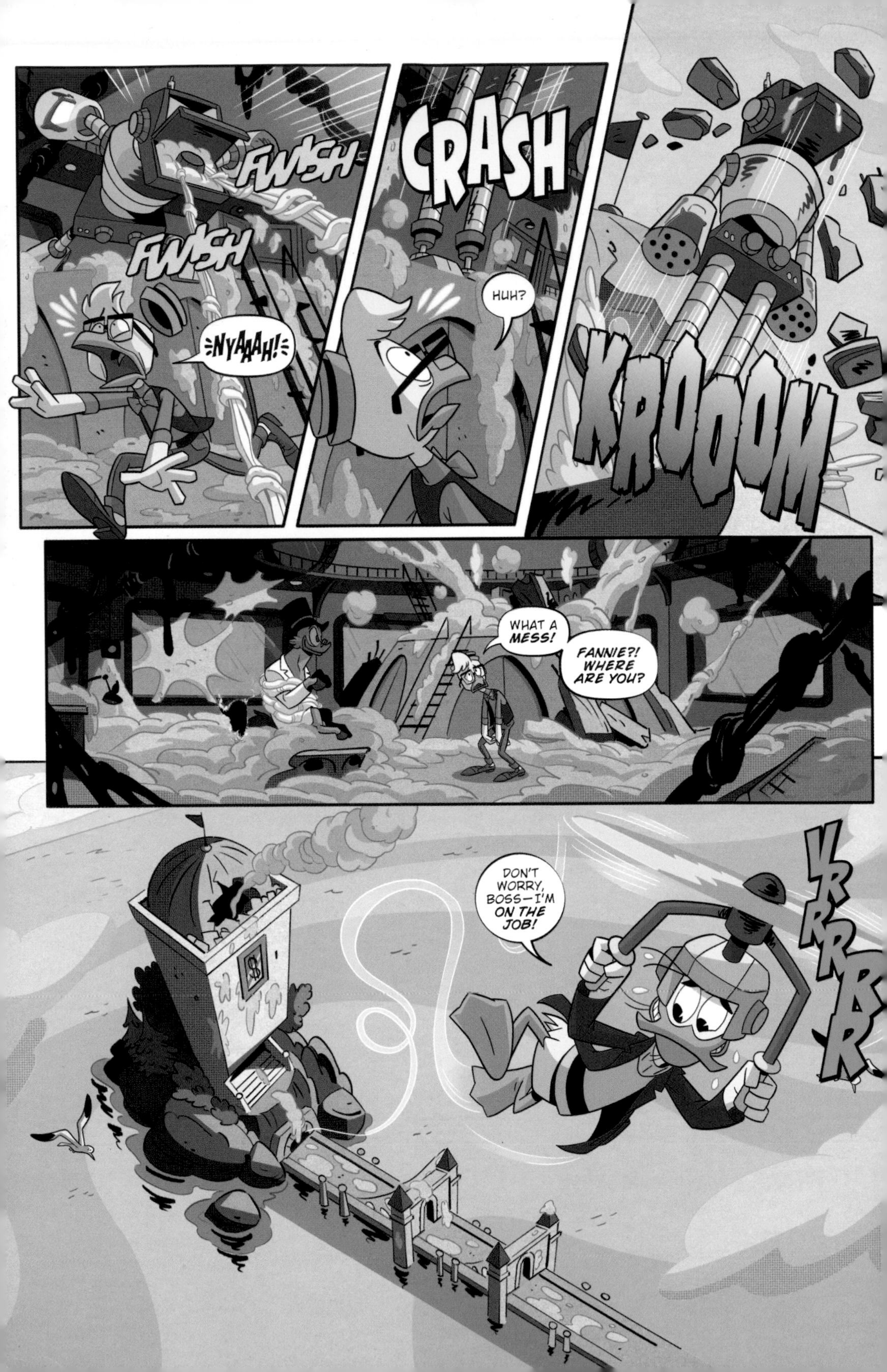
FWISH
FWISH
NYAAAH!
CRASH
HUH?
KROOOM
WHAT A MESS!
FANNIE?! WHERE ARE YOU?
DON'T WORRY, BOSS—I'M ON THE JOB!
VRRRBR

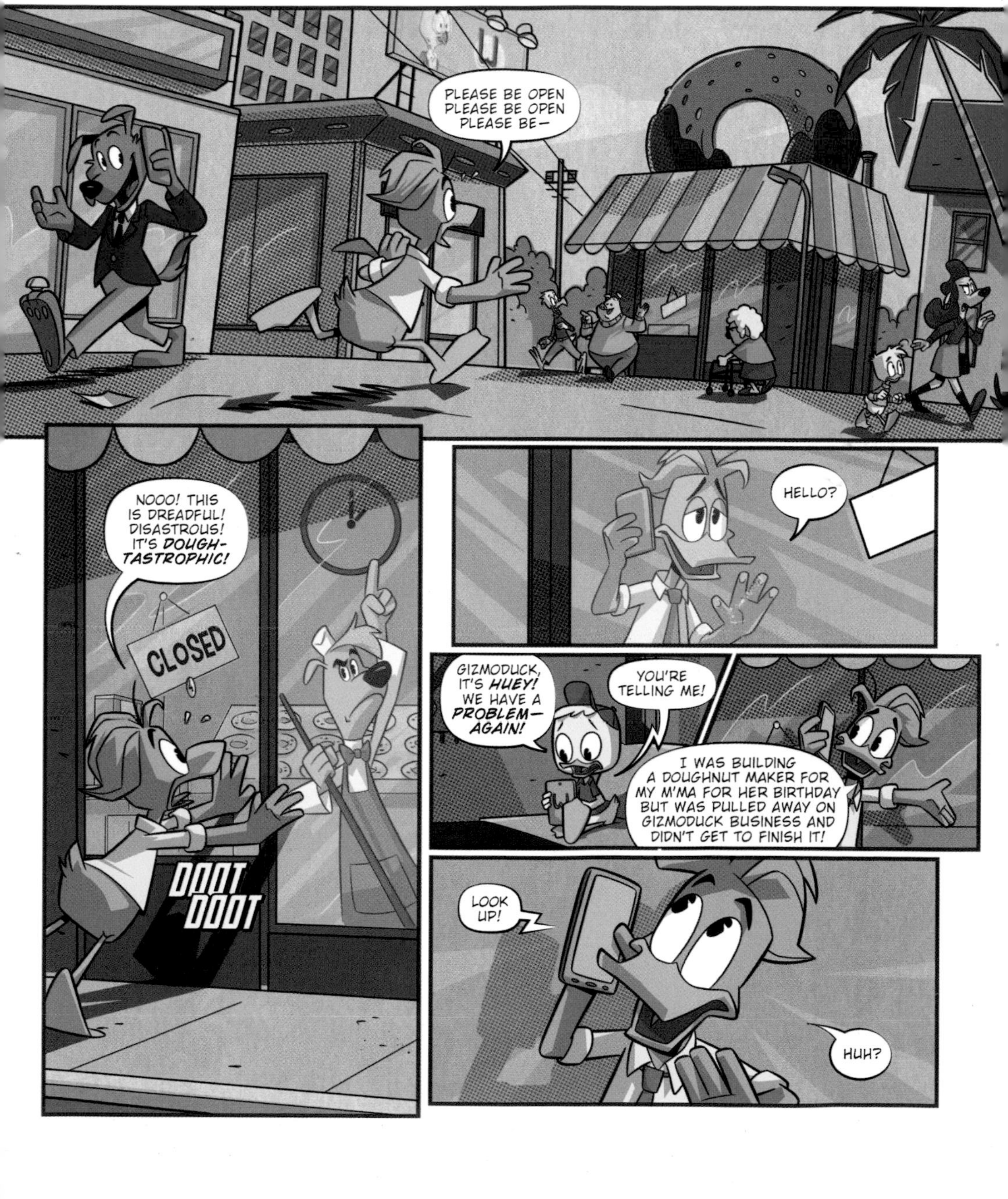
PLEASE BE OPEN PLEASE BE OPEN PLEASE BE—
NOOO! THIS IS DREADFUL! DISASTROUS! IT'S DOUGH-TASTROPHIC!
CLOSED
DOOT DOOT
HELLO?
GIZMODUCK, IT'S HUEY! WE HAVE A PROBLEM—AGAIN!
YOU'RE TELLING ME!
I WAS BUILDING A DOUGHNUT MAKER FOR MY M'MA FOR HER BIRTHDAY BUT WAS PULLED AWAY ON GIZMODUCK BUSINESS AND DIDN'T GET TO FINISH IT!
LOOK UP!
HUH?

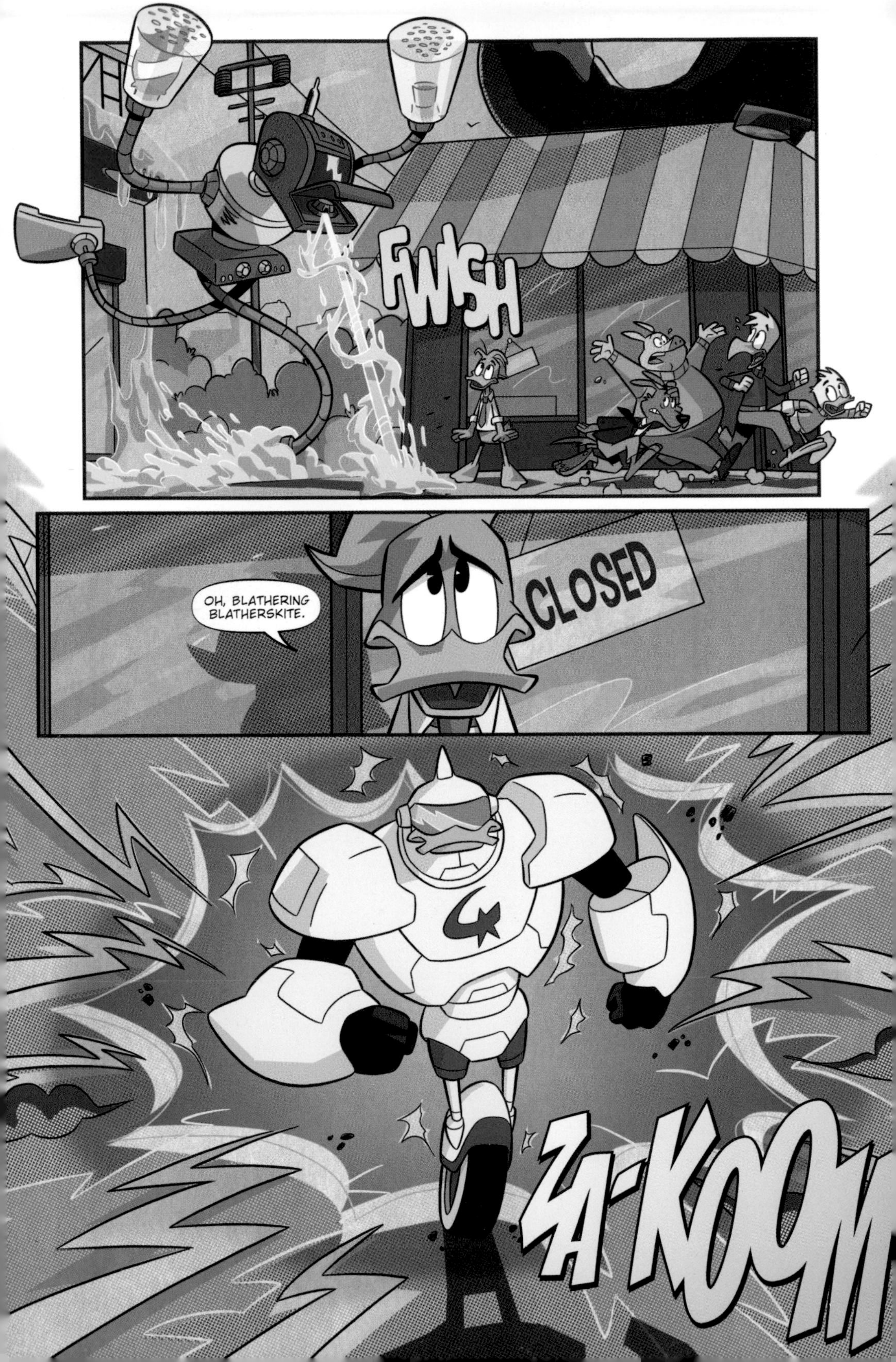
FWISH
OH, BLATHERING BLATHERSKITE.
CLOSED
ZA-KOOM

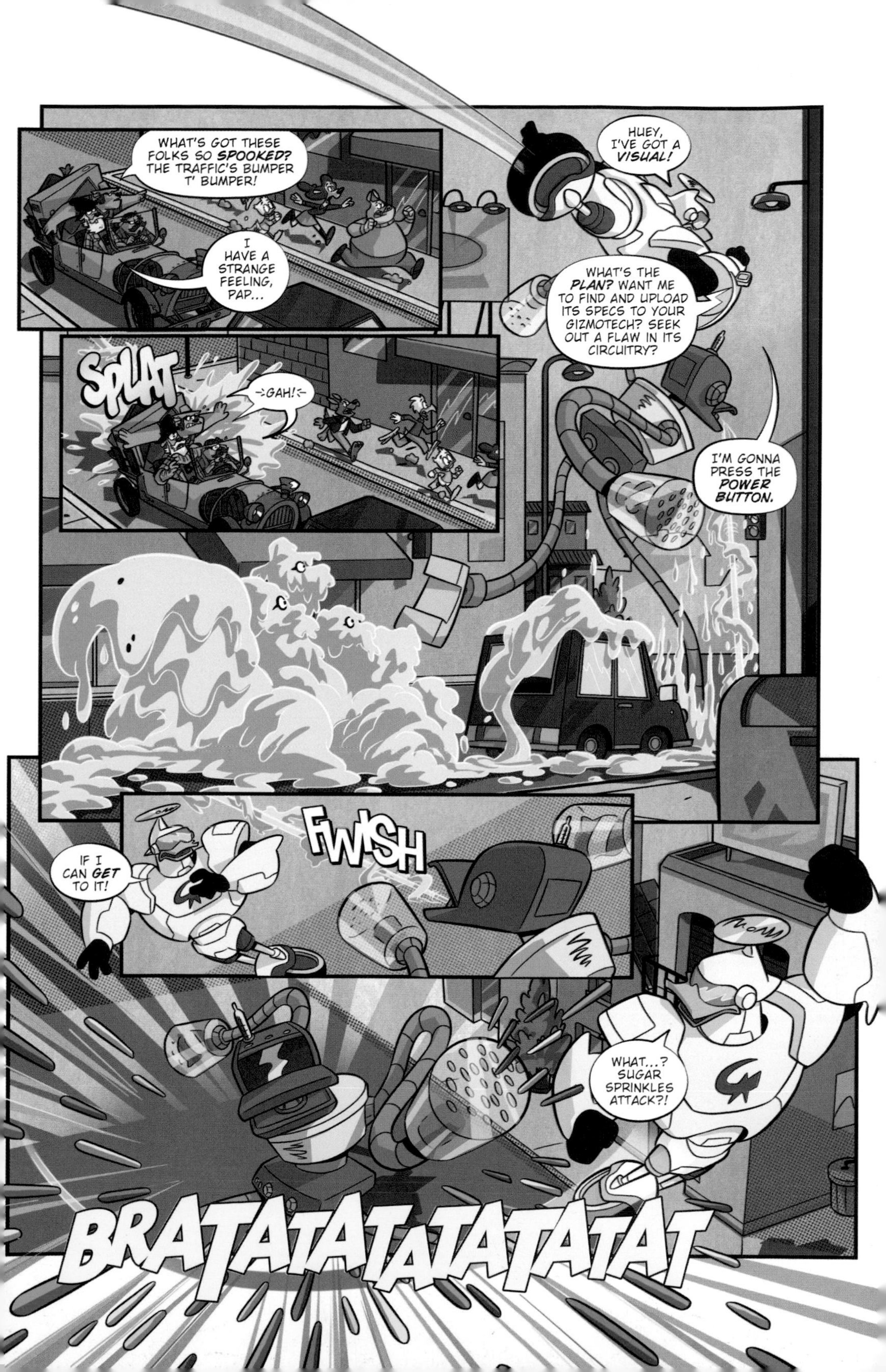
WHAT'S GOT THESE FOLKS SO SPOOKED? THE TRAFFIC'S BUMPER T' BUMPER!
I HAVE A STRANGE FEELING, PAP...
HUEY, I'VE GOT A VISUAL!
WHAT'S THE PLAN? WANT ME TO FIND AND UPLOAD ITS SPECS TO YOUR GIZMOTECH? SEEK OUT A FLAW IN ITS CIRCUITRY?
SPLAT
GAH!
I'M GONNA PRESS THE POWER BUTTON.
FWISH
IF I CAN GET TO IT!
WHAT...? SUGAR SPRINKLES ATTACK?!
BRATATATATATATAT

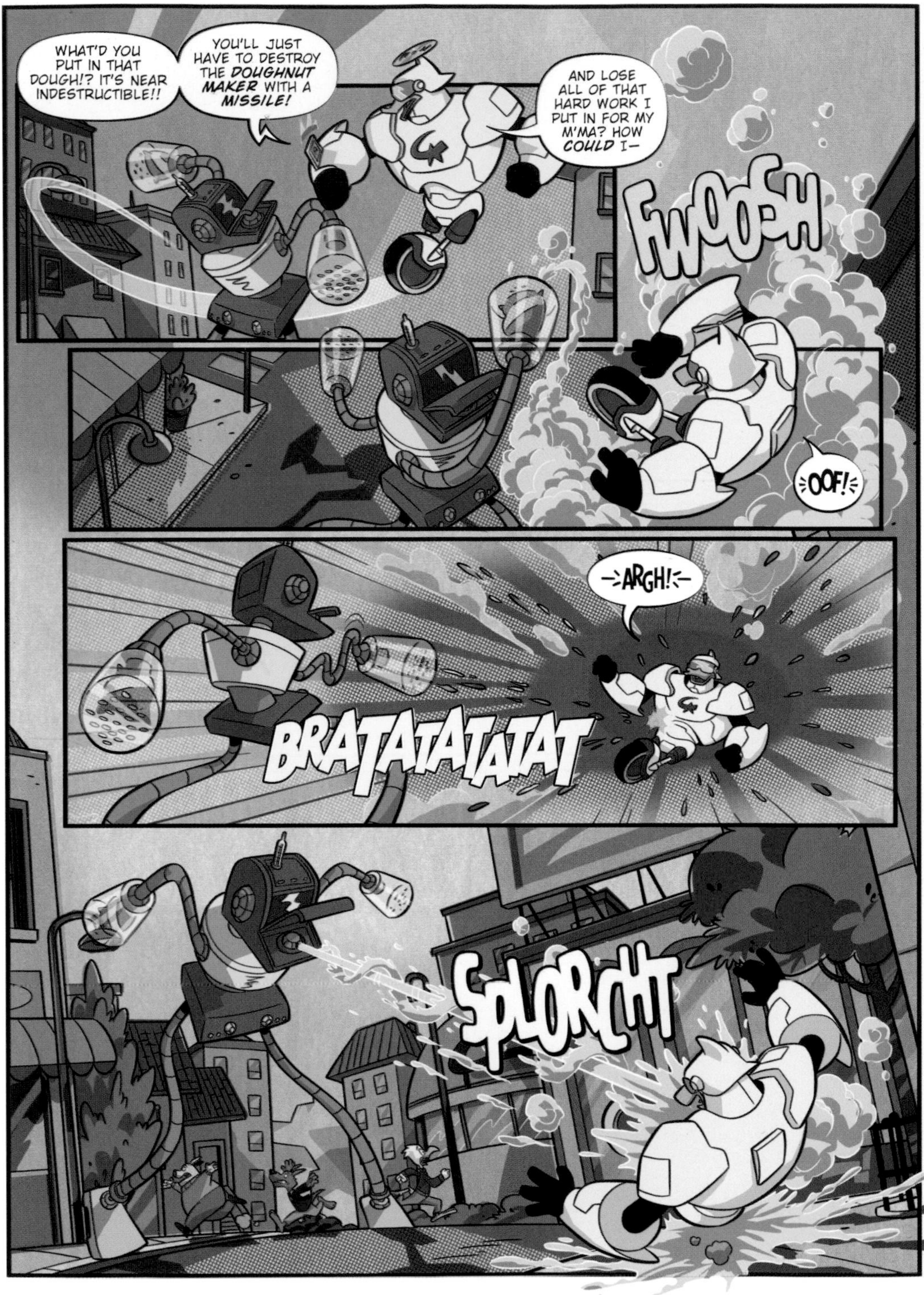
WHAT'D YOU PUT IN THAT DOUGH!? IT'S NEAR INDESTRUCTIBLE!!
YOU'LL JUST HAVE TO DESTROY THE **DOUGHNUT MAKER** WITH A **MISSILE!**
AND LOSE ALL OF THAT HARD WORK I PUT IN FOR MY M'MA? HOW **COULD** I—
FWOOSH
OOF!
ARGH!
BRATATATATAT
SPLORCHT

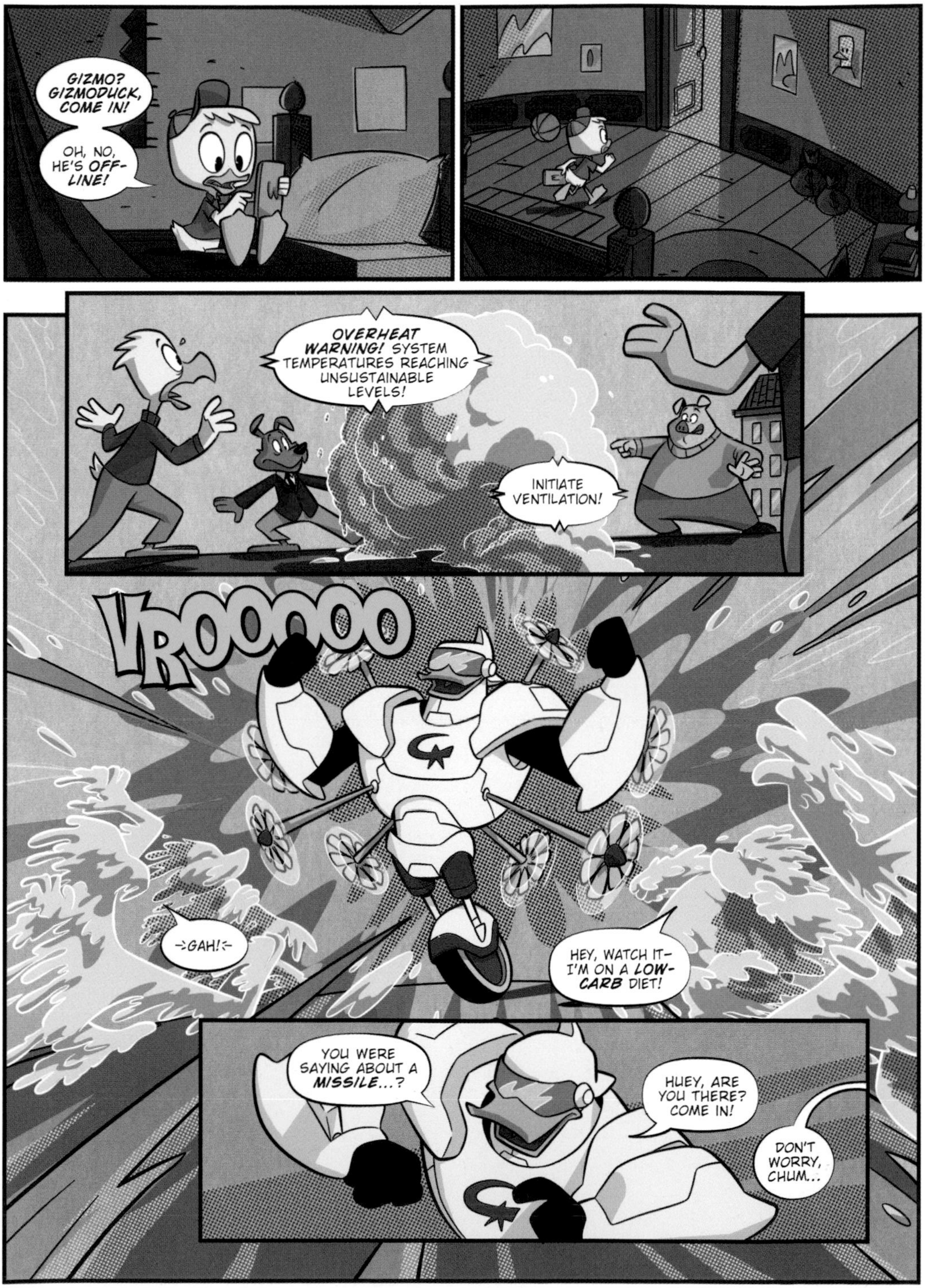
GIZMO? GIZMODUCK, COME IN!
OH, NO, HE'S OFF-LINE!
OVERHEAT WARNING! SYSTEM TEMPERATURES REACHING UNSUSTAINABLE LEVELS!
INITIATE VENTILATION!
VROOOOO
-GAH!-
HEY, WATCH IT-I'M ON A LOW-CARB DIET!
YOU WERE SAYING ABOUT A MISSILE...?
HUEY, ARE YOU THERE? COME IN!
DON'T WORRY, CHUM...

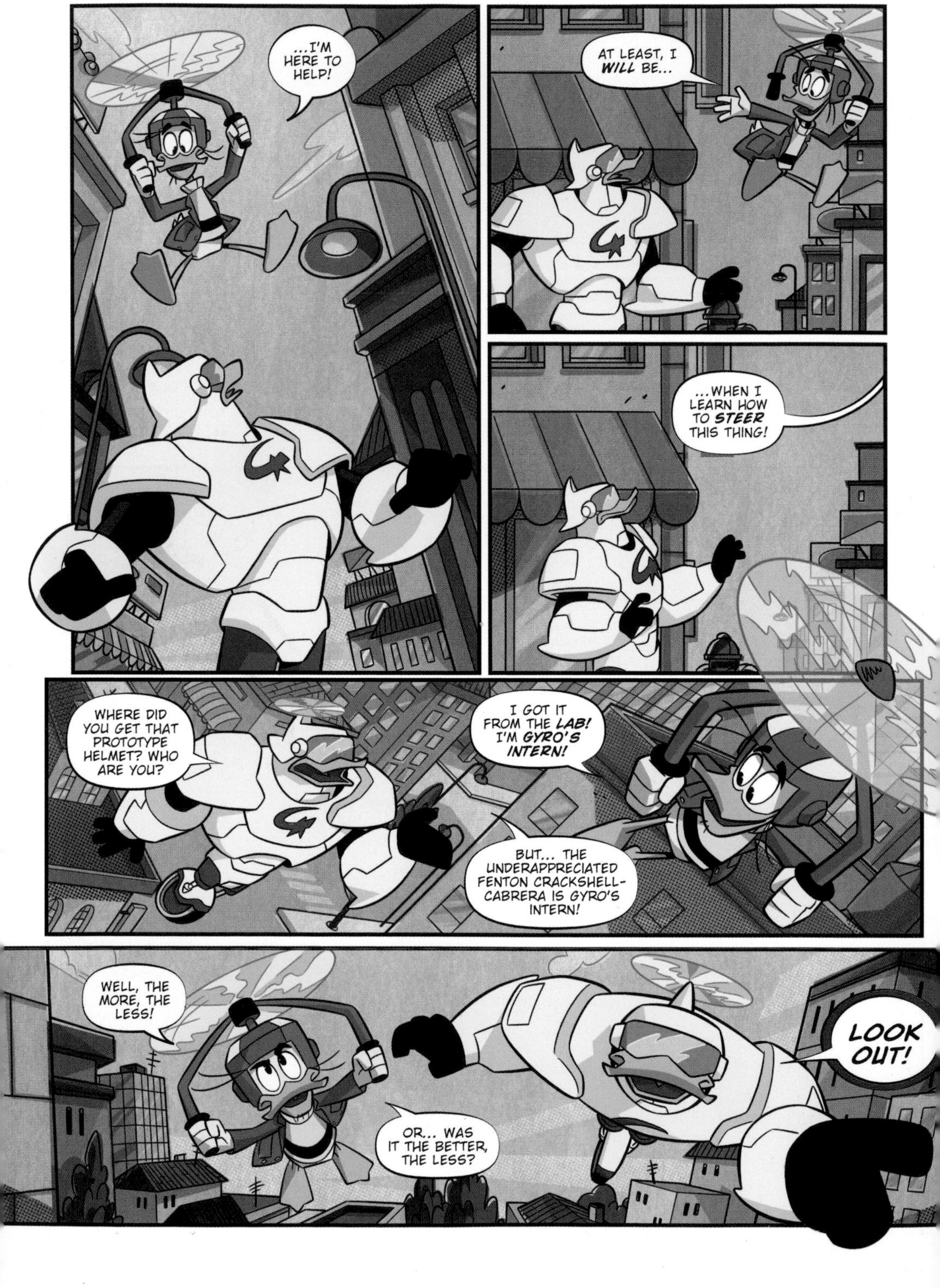
...I'M HERE TO HELP!
AT LEAST, I WILL BE...
...WHEN I LEARN HOW TO STEER THIS THING!
WHERE DID YOU GET THAT PROTOTYPE HELMET? WHO ARE YOU?
I GOT IT FROM THE LAB! I'M GYRO'S INTERN!
BUT... THE UNDERAPPRECIATED FENTON CRACKSHELL-CABRERA IS GYRO'S INTERN!
WELL, THE MORE, THE LESS!
OR... WAS IT THE BETTER, THE LESS?
LOOK OUT!

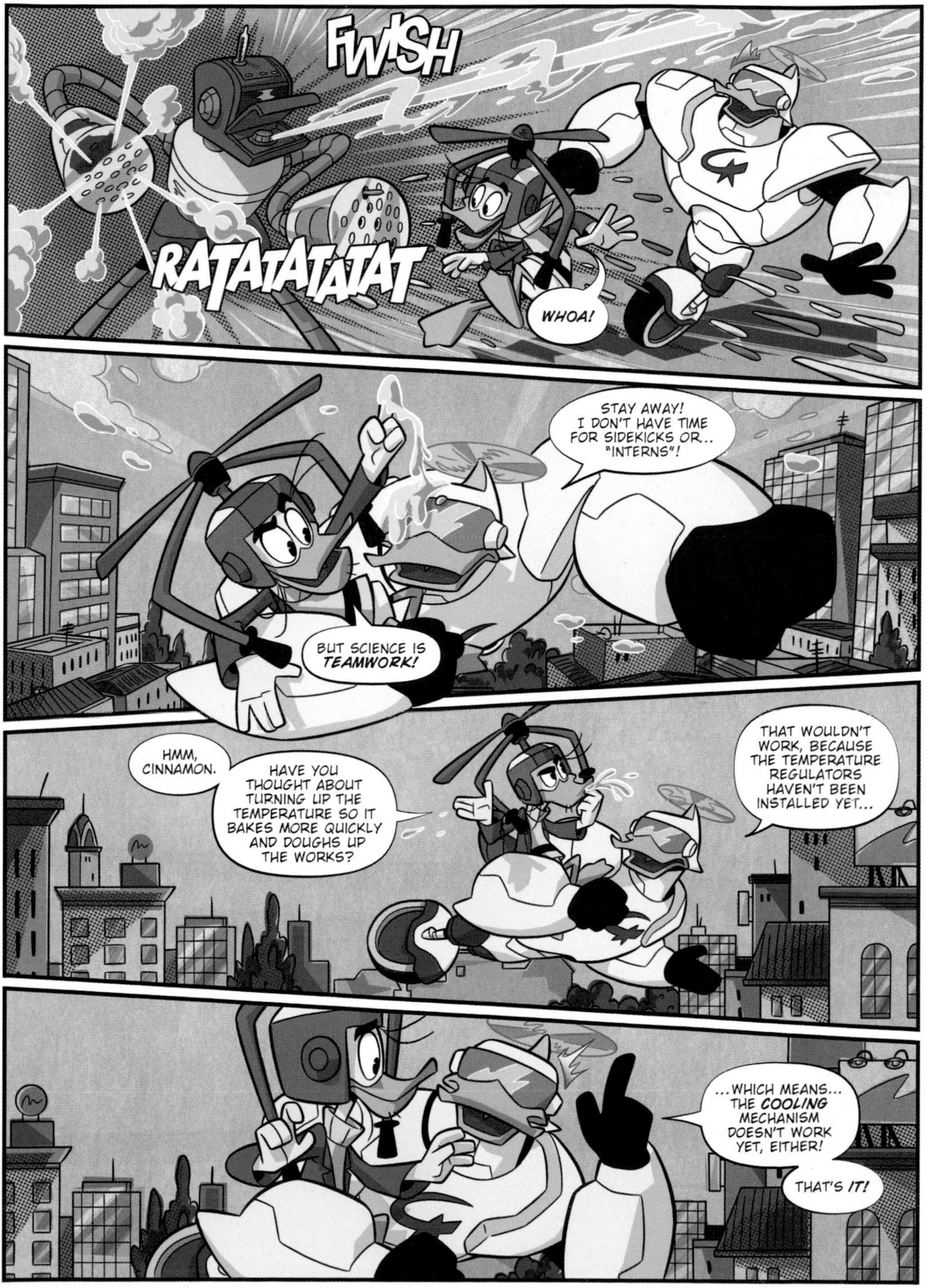
FWISH
RATATATATAT
WHOA!
STAY AWAY! I DON'T HAVE TIME FOR SIDEKICKS OR... "INTERNS"!
BUT SCIENCE IS *TEAMWORK!*
HMM, CINNAMON.
HAVE YOU THOUGHT ABOUT TURNING UP THE TEMPERATURE SO IT BAKES MORE QUICKLY AND DOUGHS UP THE WORKS?
THAT WOULDN'T WORK, BECAUSE THE TEMPERATURE REGULATORS HAVEN'T BEEN INSTALLED YET...
...WHICH MEANS... THE *COOLING* MECHANISM DOESN'T WORK YET, EITHER!
THAT'S *IT!*

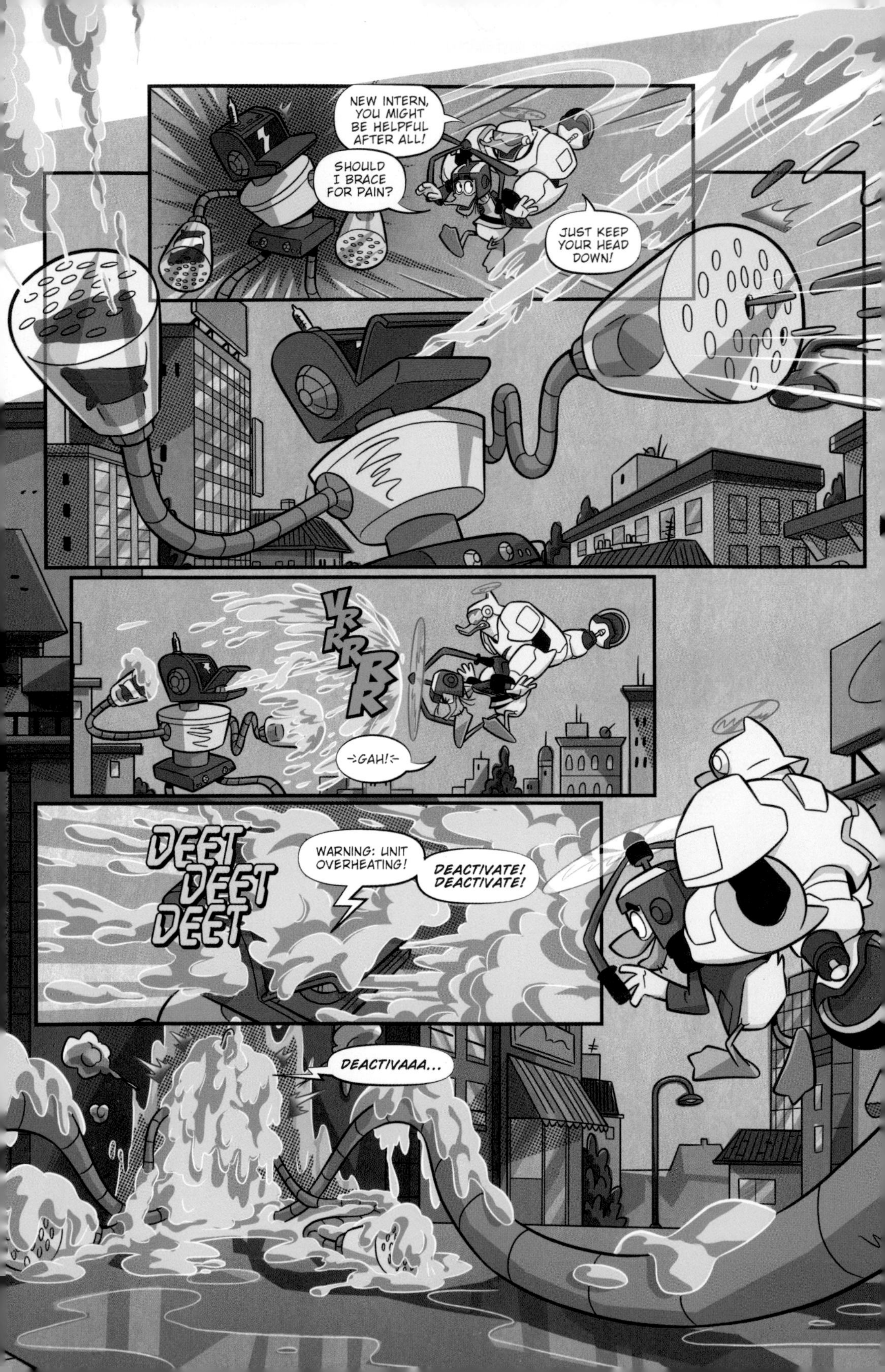
NEW INTERN, YOU MIGHT BE HELPFUL AFTER ALL!
SHOULD I BRACE FOR PAIN?
JUST KEEP YOUR HEAD DOWN!
VRRRR
GAH!
DEET DEET DEET
WARNING: UNIT OVERHEATING!
DEACTIVATE! DEACTIVATE!
DEACTIVAAA...

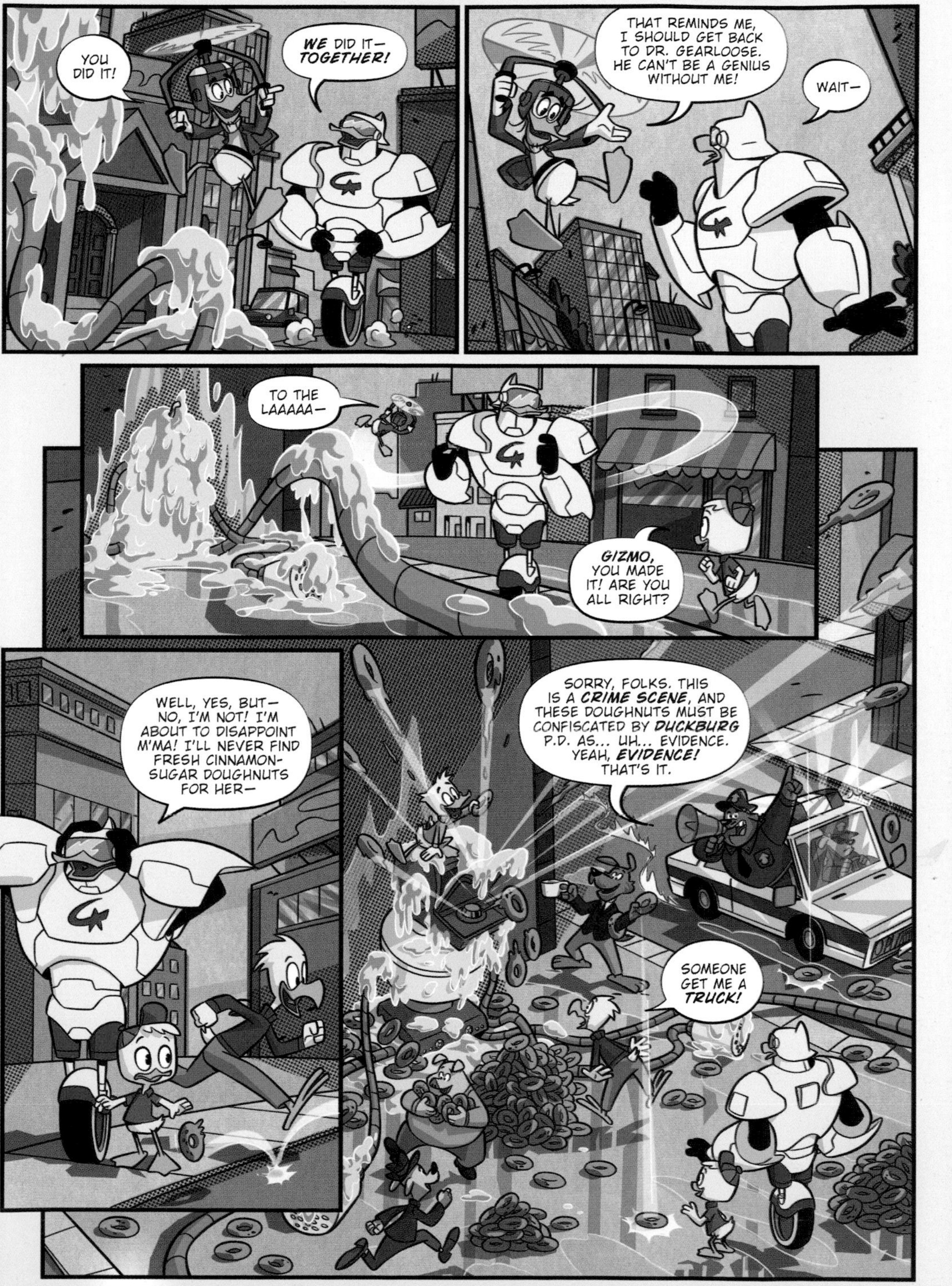
YOU DID IT!
WE DID IT— TOGETHER!
THAT REMINDS ME, I SHOULD GET BACK TO DR. GEARLOOSE. HE CAN'T BE A GENIUS WITHOUT ME!
WAIT—
TO THE LAAAAAA—
GIZMO, YOU MADE IT! ARE YOU ALL RIGHT?
WELL, YES, BUT— NO, I'M NOT! I'M ABOUT TO DISAPPOINT M'MA! I'LL NEVER FIND FRESH CINNAMON-SUGAR DOUGHNUTS FOR HER—
SORRY, FOLKS. THIS IS A CRIME SCENE, AND THESE DOUGHNUTS MUST BE CONFISCATED BY DUCKBURG P.D. AS... UH... EVIDENCE. YEAH, EVIDENCE! THAT'S IT.
SOMEONE GET ME A TRUCK!

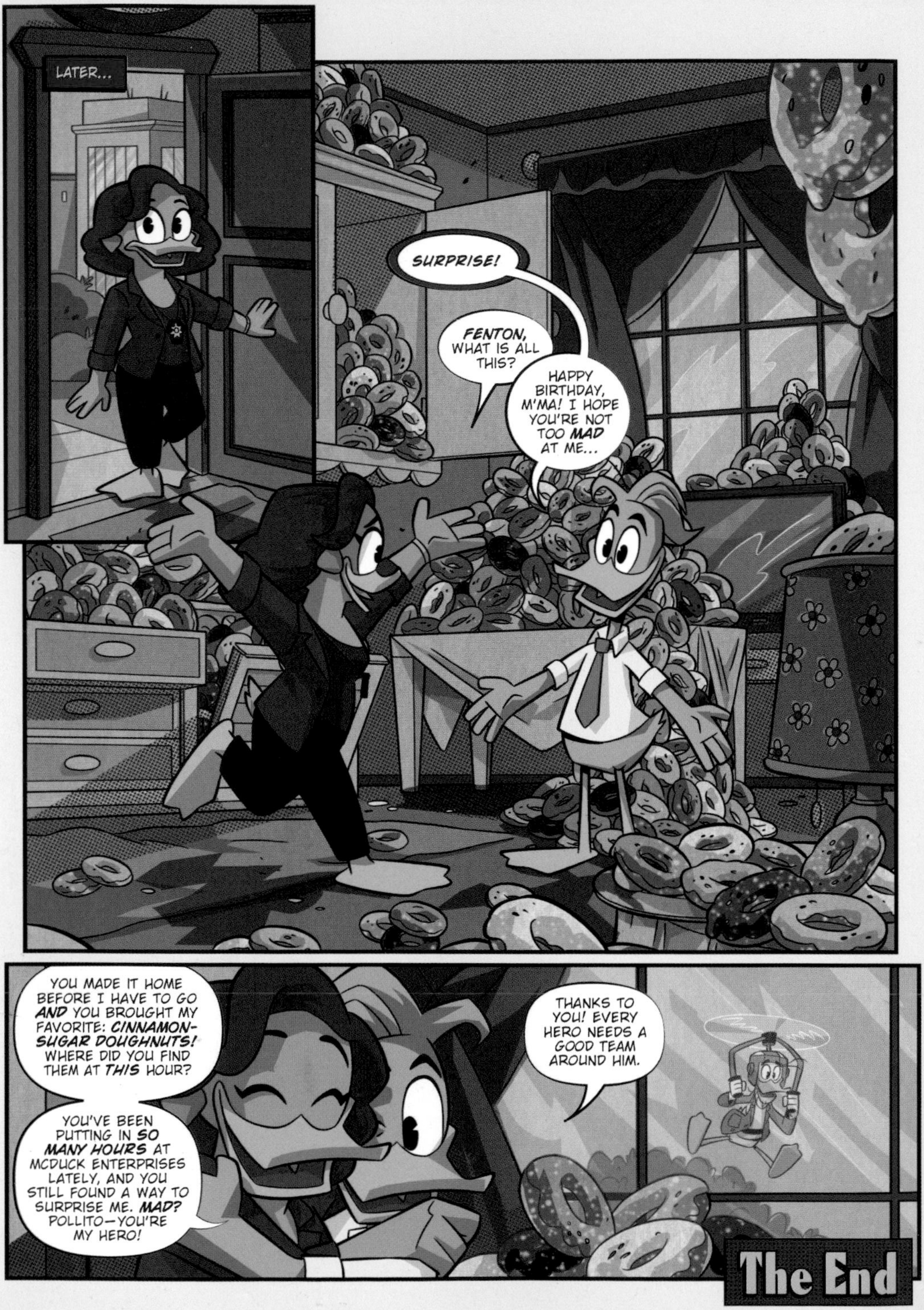
LATER...
SURPRISE!
FENTON, WHAT IS ALL THIS?
HAPPY BIRTHDAY, M'MA! I HOPE YOU'RE NOT TOO MAD AT ME...
YOU MADE IT HOME BEFORE I HAVE TO GO AND YOU BROUGHT MY FAVORITE: CINNAMON-SUGAR DOUGHNUTS! WHERE DID YOU FIND THEM AT THIS HOUR?
YOU'VE BEEN PUTTING IN SO MANY HOURS AT MCDUCK ENTERPRISES LATELY, AND YOU STILL FOUND A WAY TO SURPRISE ME. MAD? POLLITO—YOU'RE MY HERO!
THANKS TO YOU! EVERY HERO NEEDS A GOOD TEAM AROUND HIM.
The End

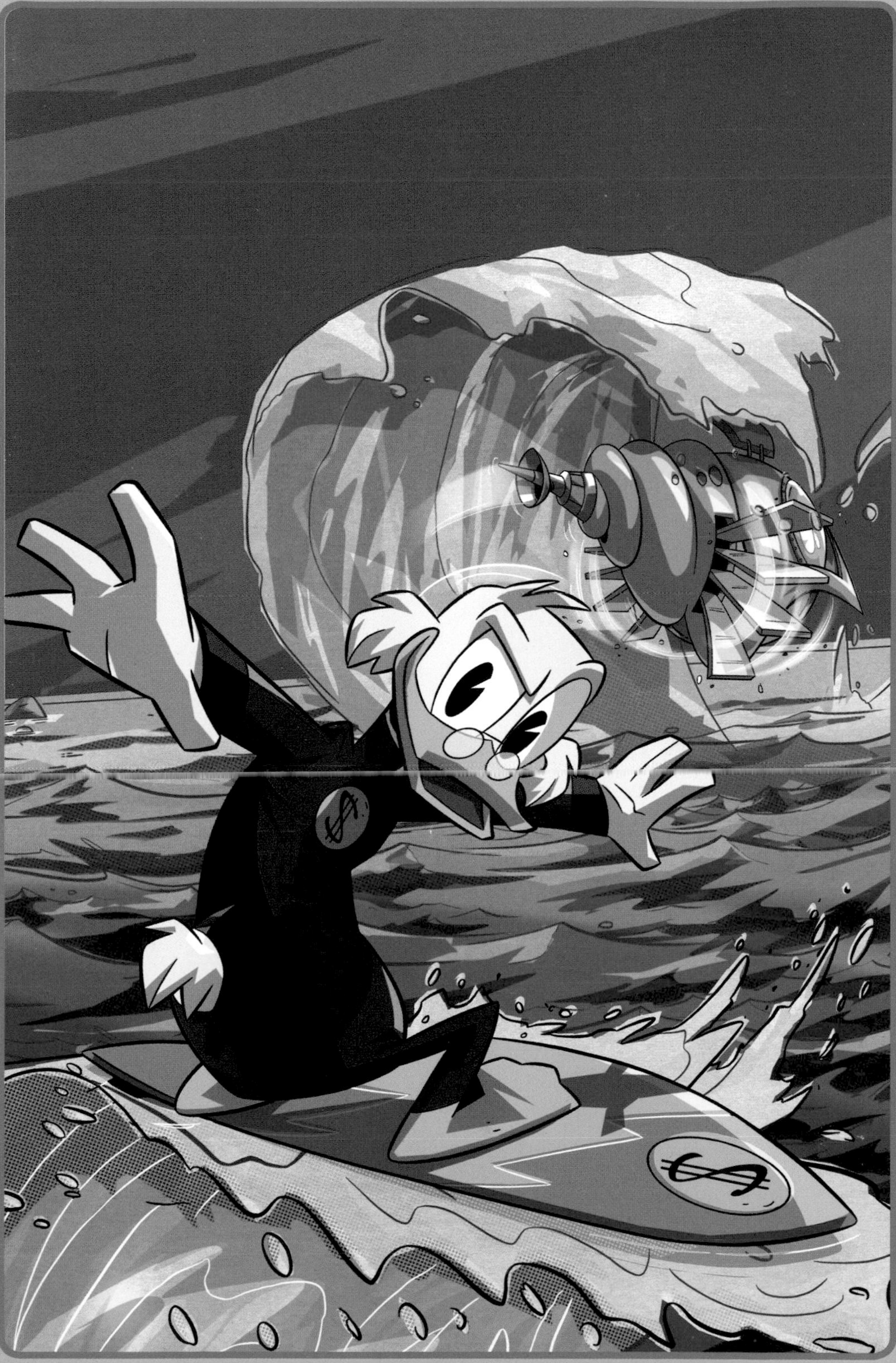

Art by Marco Ghiglione and Cristina Stella, Colors by Lucio De Giuseppe

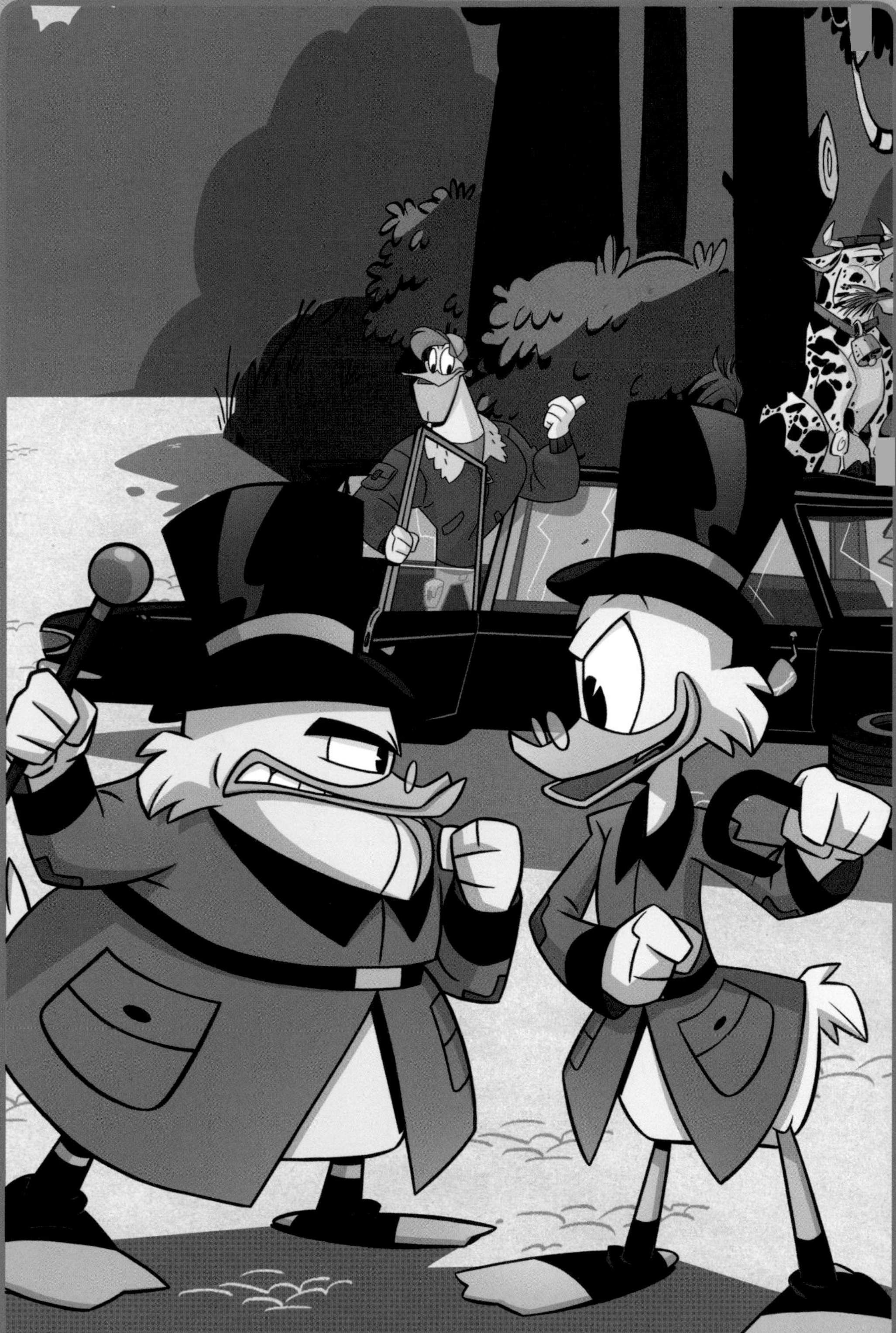

Art by Marco Ghiglione, Colors by Dario Calabria

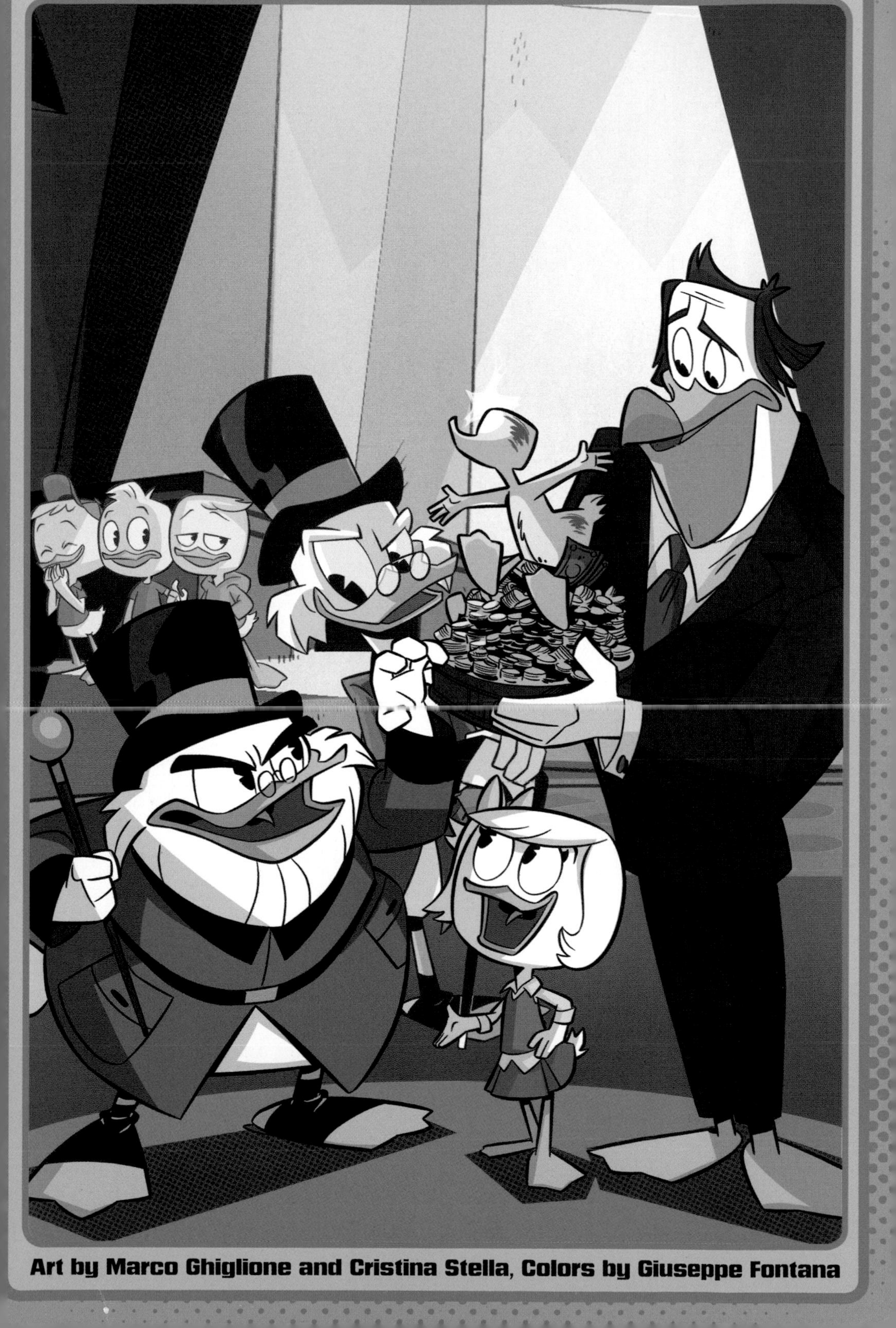

Art by Marco Ghiglione and Cristina Stella, Colors by Giuseppe Fontana

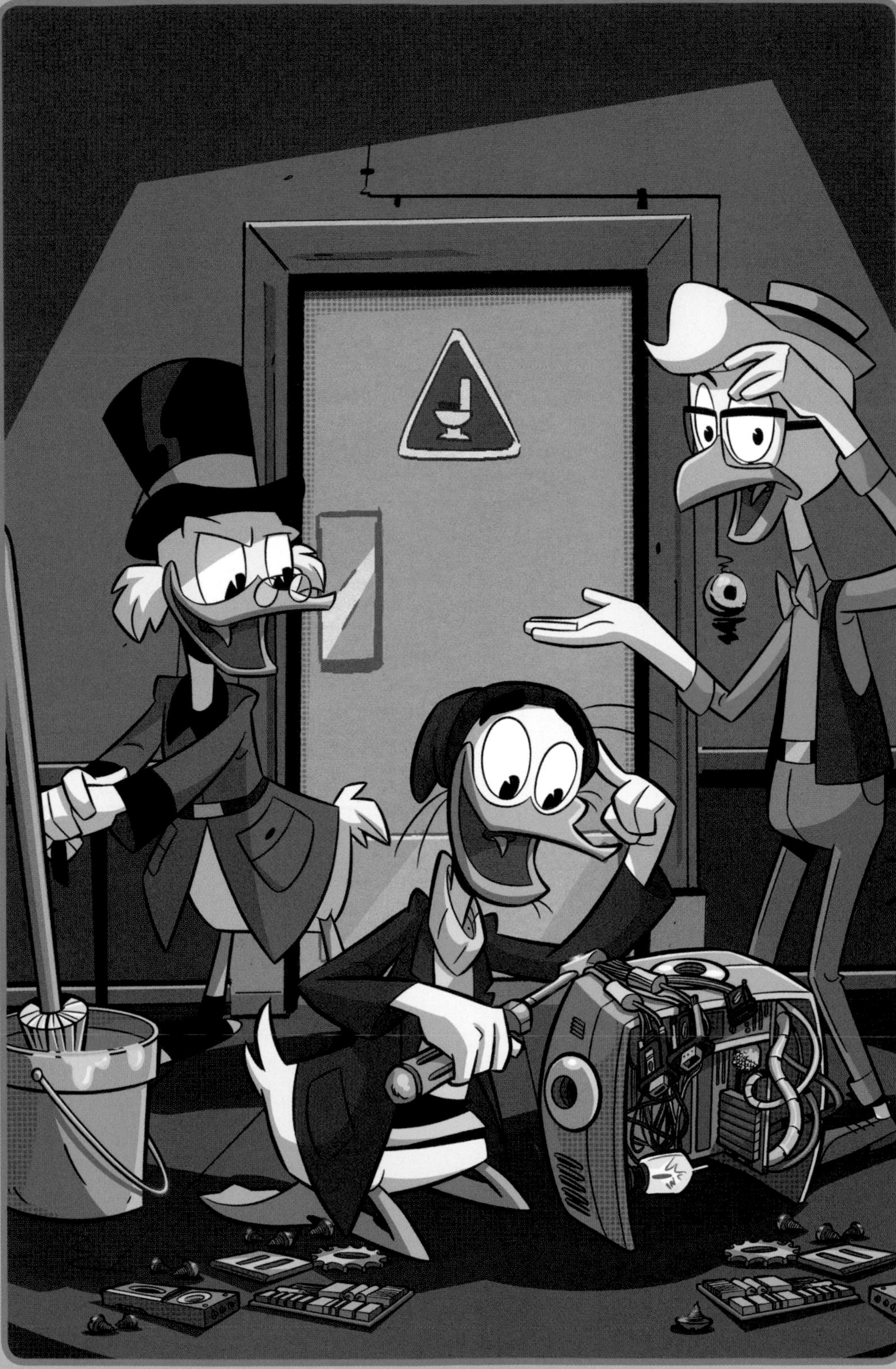

Art by Marco Ghiglione and Cristina Stella, Colors by Kawaii

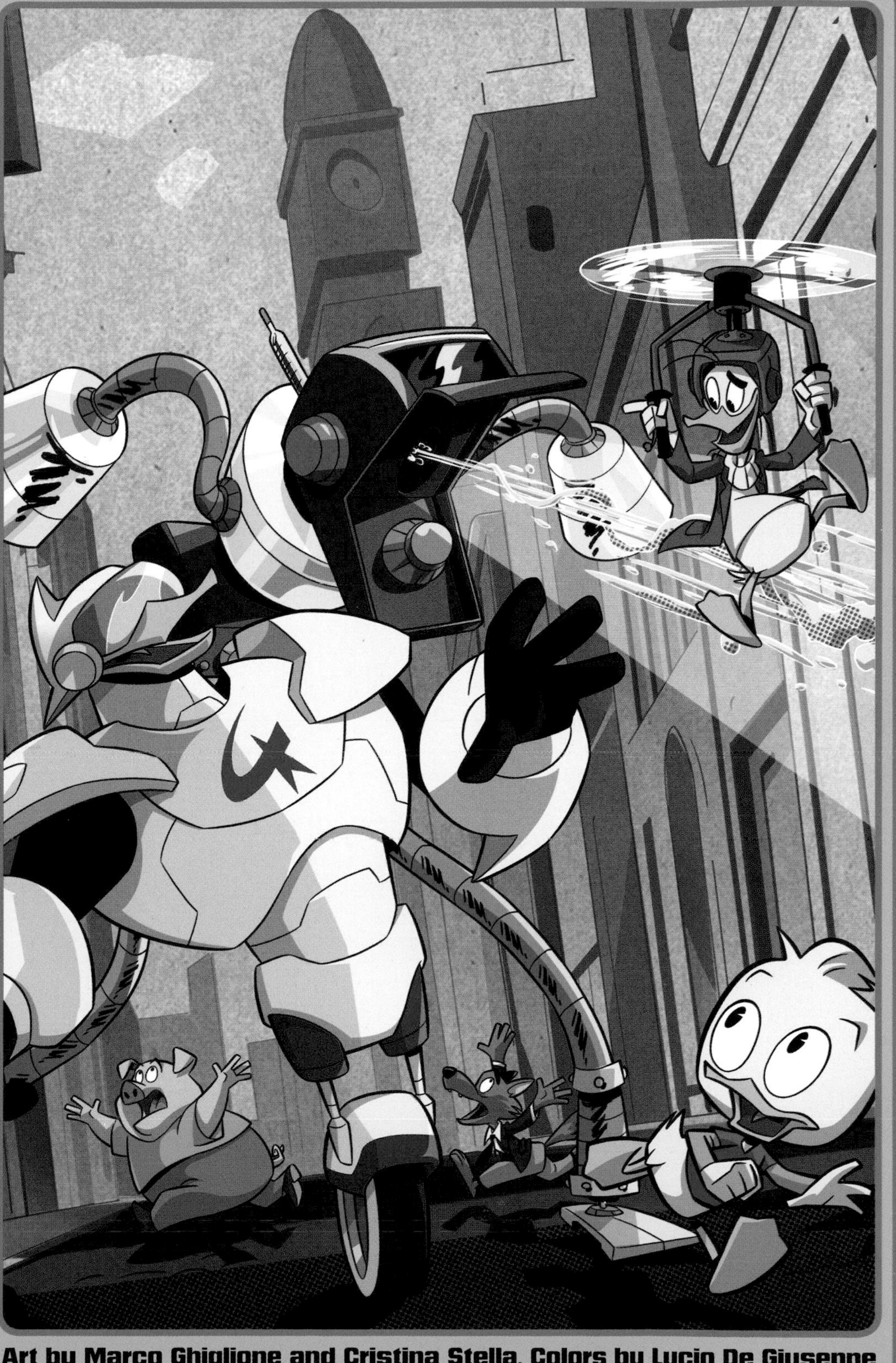

Art by Marco Ghiglione and Cristina Stella, Colors by Lucio De Giuseppe

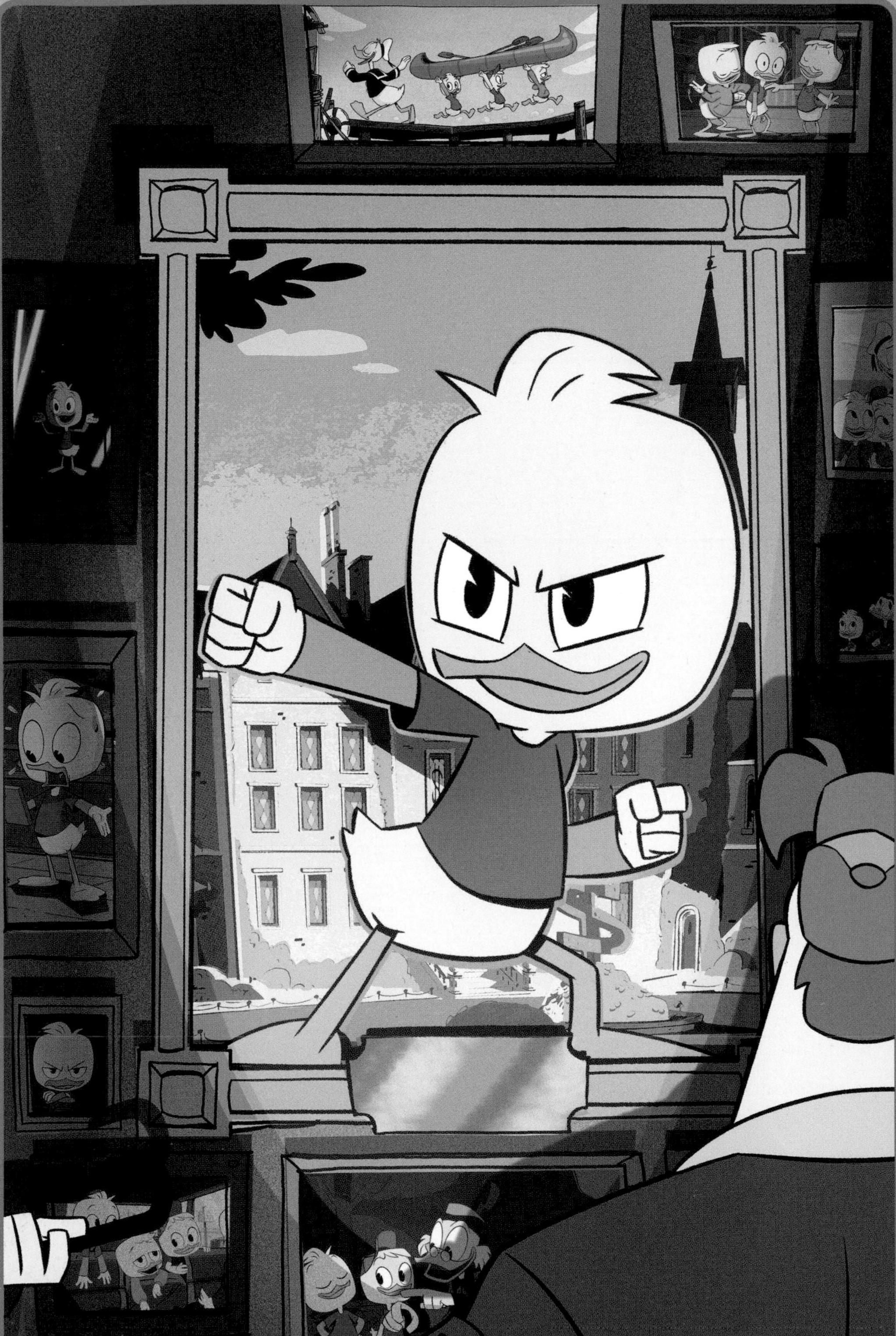

Art by DuckTales Creative Team

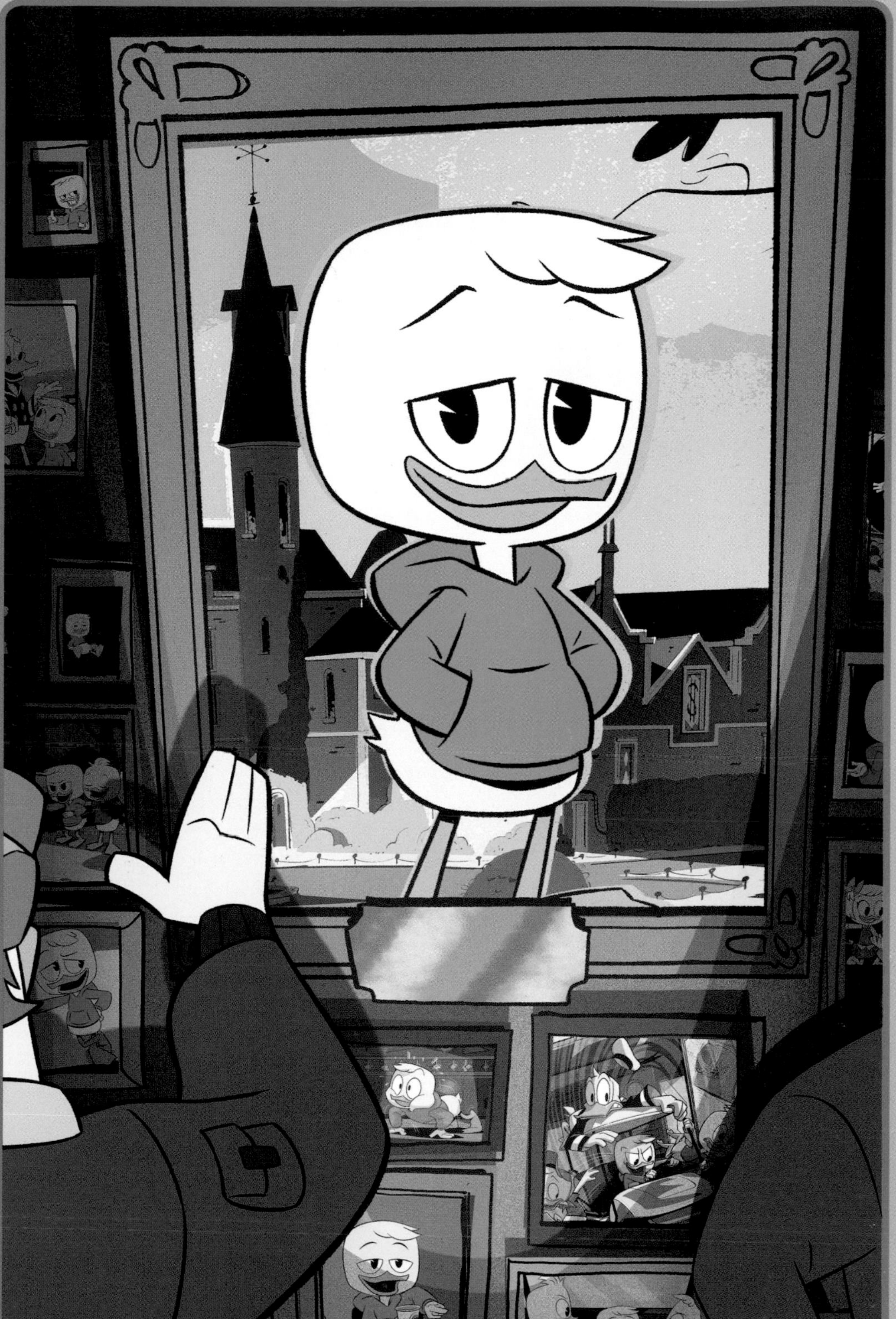

Art by DuckTales Creative Team

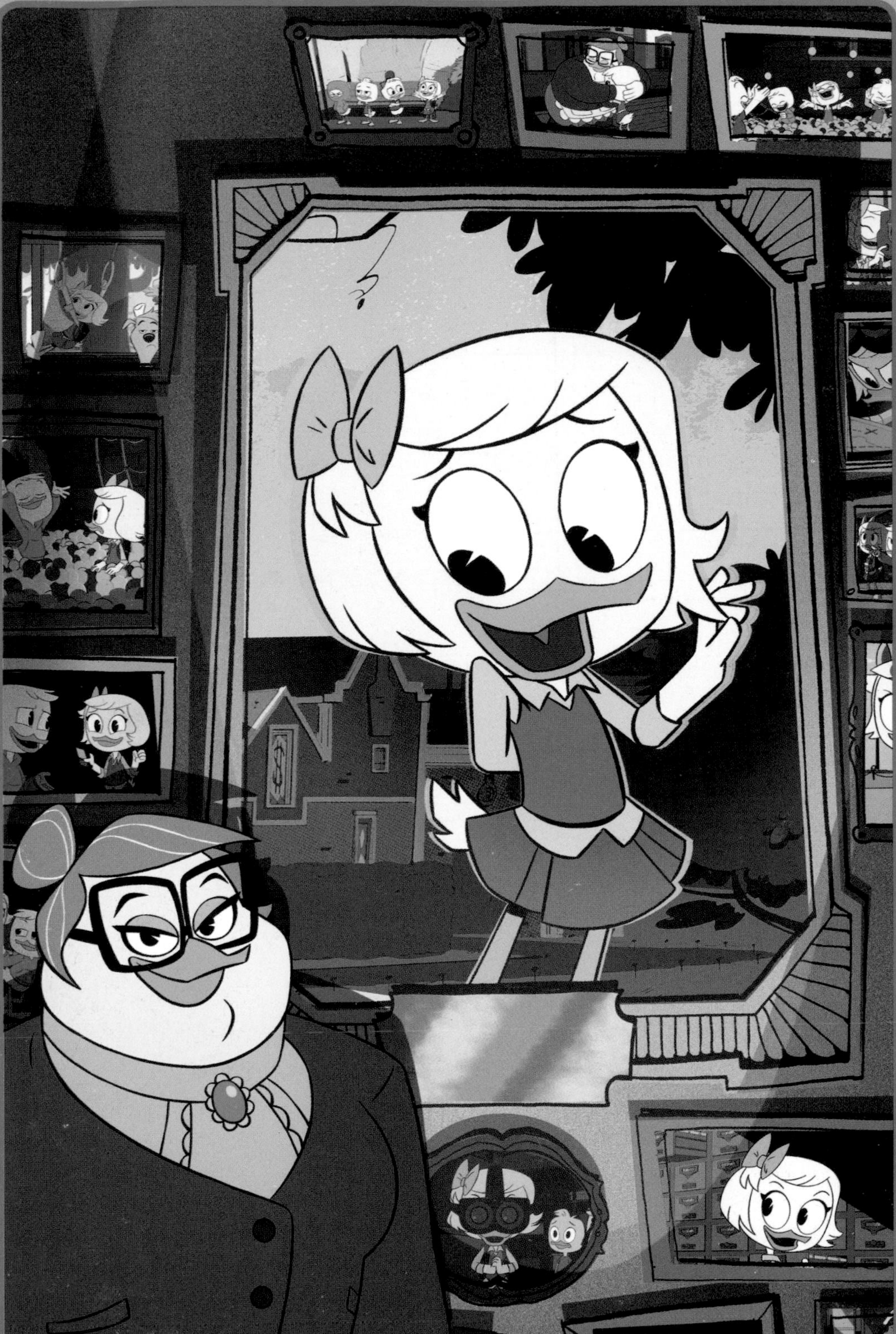

Art by DuckTales Creative Team